THE DESPERATE CHRISTMAS ANGEL

VICTORIAN ROMANCE

ELEONOR CORNISH

PUREREAD.COM

Copyright © 2023 PureRead Ltd

www.pureread.com

All rights reserved. No part of this publication may be reproduced, distributed or transmitted in any form or by any means, without prior written permission.

Publisher's Note: This is a work of fiction. Names, characters, places, and incidents are a product of the author's imagination. Locales and public names are sometimes used for atmospheric purposes. Any resemblance to actual people, living or dead, or to businesses, companies, events, institutions, or locales is completely coincidental.

CONTENTS

Dear reader, get ready for another great story…	1
Chapter 1	3
Chapter 2	14
Chapter 3	30
Chapter 4	46
Chapter 5	56
Chapter 6	70
Chapter 7	84
Chapter 8	95
Chapter 9	113
Chapter 10	123
Epilogue	129
Have you read?	135
Love Victorian Christmas Saga Romance?	151
Our Gift To You	155

DEAR READER, GET READY FOR ANOTHER GREAT STORY...

A VICTORIAN ROMANCE

With Christmas fast approaching little does Eliza Thorn realise that her straightforward life of toil and danger is about to change forever...

Turn the page and let's begin

CHAPTER 1

There was something very satisfying about the crunch underfoot as Eliza trudged over the frost-covered ground. She took a strange delight in finding small, frozen puddles and deliberately pressing on them with her boot. She did not know why, but she found a thrill in watching the ice shatter into tiny shards, discovering not a drop of liquid water beneath. The hardened mud was equally fascinating to the young girl, and she looked out for boot prints she had made in the last days. Seeing these preserved marks in the ground scattered alongside trails of water birds and the occasional fox gave the winter-locked moors a certain timeless quality, a sense of the eternal in a world that was so often changeable and impermanent.

As she trudged haphazardly over the frozen mud banks, Eliza took time to admire the shadows about her, the ghostly suggestion of dead logs, half sunk trees leaning heavily in the peat, the occasional shrub eking out a solitary existence on the scattered islands of dry ground that rose above the waterline. The thick morning fog was a constant on the moorland. In summer, the veil of mist was lit up in a golden sheen, bathing Eliza's world in an almost heavenly glow. In winter, the grey mists were almost impenetrable, Eliza's eyes only able to see twenty or thirty feet in any direction. Walking alone among the indistinct shadows made her feel like she was moving through some waking dream state, everything insubstantial and ethereal except for her. Some would have found the shrouded isolation of the moors depressing, melancholic, but not Eliza. She found the barely navigable and ever-changing waterways exciting, calling to her sense of adventure and discovery as she charted her way through the unmapped fog.

An expert in judging the ground beneath her, Eliza made her way across the boggy ground without once slipping into the ice filmed water or straying onto a damp patch of mud that had not yet frozen over. Eliza prided herself on how well she moved across the quagmire, claiming often that she was lighter than air to her younger brother who lacked the balance and shrewd eye to make it across the bogs.

Coming to a suitable place to begin her work, Eliza shrugged off the large satchel she carried, laying it down on the firm, frozen grasses where she stood. Then, bending down, she tested the mud around her. The slight sheen on the surface suggested the ground was still damp and she nodded approvingly as her finger sank easily into the cold muck. She withdrew her hand and wiped the dirt off on a rag she had stuffed away in her bag. Taking off her coat and laying it down by her pack, Eliza shuddered momentarily from the cold that nipped at her. She rubbed her arms and blew out a sigh, watching as the steam carried from her lips onto the frostbitten air. The cold was something she would simply have to endure for a time, and the small girl tried to reassure herself that her coat would feel all the warmer when she put it on again.

Rolling up the sleeves of her dress, Eliza once again returned to her knees, leaning as far over the damp mud as she dared without risking falling in. She bunched up her face, lips disappearing altogether as she drove her arms deep into the mud.

The liquid ooze was thick and cold. Eliza did not much care for it in any season, but winter was by far the most testing time for her. She drove her arms in up to the elbows then became still as she let herself adjust to the cold bite of the muck and stagnant water pooled around her. To help with the process, she looked up, staring into the fog and enjoying, once again, the ethereal shadows that surrounded her on all sides. She could see the curtain-like branches of an old willow somewhere ahead, the tree looking like a long-necked woman with her hair cascading down into the water. Elsewhere, a wood pigeon could be heard calling out through the gloom. Narrowing her eyes and focusing a little harder still, Eliza was sure she could see the distinctive spindle legs and noble frame of a heron trudging slowly through the mud, questing through the mire for some fish or perhaps a hibernating frog to enjoy for its breakfast.

At last, the chill bite of the muddy water subsided, and Eliza felt able to begin her work. Pulling her arms out of the water, she grabbed a jar from her satchel and then plunged it deep into the water. This time, she pushed her arms even further into the muck, trying to reach the very bottom. She scooped the thickest mud into the jar and then hauled her arms out. It was hard going. The thick mud held her fast, a horrible wet sound echoing across the wetlands as she fought the suction. At last, though, she pulled herself free and was able to pour the mud out onto the bank beside her. She spread the muck thin over the frosted grass, smiling with relief as she immediately spotted three black, blob-like entities that lay dormant and still among the ooze.

Leeches.

Opening up a second jar, Eliza deposited the three leeches inside, leaving the lid open. The tiny parasites inside did not move at all, each frozen in winter hibernation, which was exactly how Eliza liked them.

Leech picking was no job for the faint of heart. No matter the season, there was always some element of the job to be reviled and hated. In winter, it was the cold and chill of working in the icy waters that got to Eliza. However, at least in those months, the Leeches were nothing more than jewelled blobs she had to dig out of the mud where they slept. In summer, leeching was a good deal easier and a good deal more painful at once. In the warmer months, when the foul parasites were active in the waters, Eliza had to use her own body as bait to catch the little bloodsuckers. She would wade out into the shallow waters and simply wait for the leeches to become attracted to her. They would latch onto her flesh with their cruel jaws, their body's pulsating and fattening as they sucked her blood. She would pull each one off her body and deposit them in a jar just as she was doing now, but the act of pulling the lock-jawed creatures from her flesh was always painful. Even after years at the work, Eliza still felt a sharp sting every time one of the bloodsuckers attached themselves to her and every time she pried them off her.

Shuddering as a stiff breeze whipped through the willows and across her back, Eliza tried to remember the pains of hunting for leeches in the summer, reassuring herself that she was better off frozen and bite-free than warm and riddled with marks all down her legs.

The morning's work was favourable for Eliza. As the sun rose and the mists that surrounded the waters eased, she felt quite confident she would be finished with her grim duty before afternoon. Mr Barrows, the village doctor, would be impressed with her time and the number of leeches she had collected over the morning—three jars full. Buoyed by her success, Eliza allowed herself a moment of repose, pulling her arms out of the mud and resting on the banks for a few minutes. Common sense told her she would be better off finishing her work. The sooner she topped off her last jar with leeches for the doctor, the sooner she could be home and warming by the fire. Still, Eliza wanted the break, and she enjoyed the views of the still, quiet moorland that stretched out before her. At least, the moors were almost still.

Somewhere farther away in the thinning mists, Eliza spied a figure moving through the mud. She could not make out any details, just a shadow, arms spread wide and stance constantly shifting. No doubt, whoever the explorer of the bogs was, they were unused to moving over the shifting mud. The heron that had spent the morning prowling the waters took to the air, angered by the interruption the blustering interloper was causing. Eliza frowned, watching the shadow closer as it seemed to struggle to find its way. She knew almost all the fishermen, fellow leech collectors and ramblers who wandered the fenlands, and none of them would have so hard a time navigating the mud. She could only assume, whoever was ahead of her was new to the task and she could not help but worry.

Twice in quick succession, the shadow seemed to dip, a poorly placed foot sinking into the mud and threatening to send the shadow falling into the mire. Each time, the shadow righted itself, but Eliza's fears were growing moment by moment. There were not many accidents or deaths recorded out on the fens, but they were not unheard of either. Almost always they involved some drunkard or a bold fool who had ventured out across the swamp without fully appreciating the dangers and challenges the wetlands posed.

Eliza's body was tense, and she knew she could not return to her work while some idiot was blustering about and at risk of harming themselves. Forgetting the possibility of an early finish and the fire of home, Eliza resolved to leave her pack and jars and go to the stranger's aid. However, just as she stood and looked to ensure her things were secure, a cry caused her to look up with fearful eyes. The shadow was gone, disappeared beneath the waters.

Young Edward Stanford had stormed off onto the fens without much preparation or forethought. Impetuous by nature, governed by his heart rather than his head, he could have done little less when his elder brother had dared him to venture out across the wetlands and bring back a toad as proof of his success.

Edward was in a long and protracted war with his brother —at least he saw it that way. Martin was always crowing about his rank and seniority as the elder brother, always eager to remind his little brother how his fortunes would rise and fall on his say so. In Martin's mind, Edward was little more than a glorified servant of the household, someone to boss about and order as he saw fit. If Edward objected, Martin would remind his little brother of his place and recite again all he could do in adulthood to make his life a misery.

Of course, Edward did not stand easily for his brother's jibes and threats. Though young, he was not to be intimidated by those older or bigger than him. It had led to more than a few tousles between the lads, Edward inevitably leaving the fight with a bruise or black eye. When their mother had intervened and finally warned Martin to watch his manners around his younger brother, Martin had found a new way to keep his irksome pest of a sibling at bay…. dares.

Whenever Martin did not wish to be bothered by Edward or felt a need to punish his younger brother for some misdeed or other, Martin would invent some new dare and 'test of courage' for Edward to overcome to prove himself a man. In the last six months, he had his little brother climbing the tallest tree on the estate and stranding himself in its upper boughs, spending the night in the hayloft of the stables and bringing their mother into a frightened panic when it seemed her youngest had run away from home, and even had Edward steal their father's gold-plated pen from his office. That last hiding had earned Edward a severe rap across the knuckles and Mr

Stanford had all but denied his existence for a good fortnight afterward.

Now, Edward had been convinced to embark on another quest to prove himself: to venture out into the frozen, winter-locked waters of the mudflats and find a hibernating toad. Once again, Edward had fallen for his brother's mischief and, once again, put himself in greater danger than he had first realised.

"Wow, this bog is wetter than I thought. Mother is going to kill me when she sees the state of my boots... I'll have to wash them in the servants' entryway and claim the dogs dragged them out in the snow..." Edward spoke to no one in particular as he trudged over the narrow patches of dry ground before him. The winter's cold nipped at him fiercely, his feet particularly feeling the effects after having been submerged up to the knees thrice already since he had started his journey. Mumbling incoherently to himself helped steel his courage, helped him to ignore the trials of the wetlands and keep himself centered on the task before him.

It was only now, deep into the boggy mire and thoroughly lost, that Edward even realised he had no idea where to search for a hibernating frog or toad. Should he be digging in the mud with his hands, or looking for mounds of leaf litter? Only brought out into the country for holidays, Edward knew little of the wildlife outside his home. He could no more recite the hibernation habits of a toad than he could tell a toad from a frog. Still, his brother had worked his way under his skin again, and Edward was determined not to return home until he had found a toad and presented it to Martin.

The further Edward ventured, the narrower and sparser the sections of dry, solid earth became. It felt like he was hop-stepping between little islands that poked out of the waters, and the frozen mud he had encountered on the edges of the wetlands had now turned wet and sludgy in these deeper recesses.

Mis-stepping twice more, Edward grumbled to himself as he hauled his left foot out of the boggy ground. The suction around his leg was incredible and he had to put real effort into pulling his leg free of the mire. He feared his boot being lost altogether and having to hop home on only one leg. However, when his leg became trapped a second time, his fears took on a more ominous turn.

As Edward's left leg sank up to his knee once more in the boggy swamp, he felt an even greater resistance as he tried to right himself. This time, he feared he was truly stuck in the mud and stranded all alone out on the fens. Panicked and yet still determined not to be defeated by the mire, Edward began to throw his whole weight this way and that, twisting his torso and reaching out to grab the roots of a nearby tree to use as an anchor as he attempted to free himself from the mud's wet clutches. He succeeded.

Throwing his weight all on one side and pulling on the tree root with all his might, Edward Stanford succeeded in hauling his leg out of the mire. However, the surprise of being free, and the lack of resistance against him, caused him to overbalance yet again. Thrown by the momentum and horribly unbalanced, Edward's body spanned over the narrow stretch of dry ground on which he stood. Time seemed to slow, and Edward seemed intensely aware of everything around him as he felt his balance tip and his whole body fall out into the deeper stretch of icy water on the farther side of him. He felt only momentary resistance against his back as the ice that frosted over the waters shattered around him. Then, all the boy knew was cold.

CHAPTER 2

Eliza had her skirts hiked up, mud and dirty water dirtying her stockings and boots as she plunged through the mists to get to the shadow that had fallen into the water. Ordinarily, she could navigate the bogs without getting a single stain on her, but when every second might be the difference between rescue and death, she had no time to check her footing. She had enough intuition and presence of mind to avoid the worst of the pitfalls, ensuring she did not become trapped in the mud as the stranger had done several times before finally falling into the waters.

As she neared the spot where the poor unfortunate soul had fallen Eliza was relieved to see she was well in time to perform a rescue. Though there was no sign of the man above the waterline, the water all about was frothing and swirling wildly as the stranger thrashed amongst the reeds and mud. Eliza breathed an urgent prayer for strength, and dropped down to her knees, hands reaching into the dark, murky waters and groping blindly until she felt something hard brush against her fingers. She seized it, relief filling her when she realised she had caught the stranger by the wrists. His fingers wrapped around hers and she began to pull, careful to keep her grip on the solid earth lest she be dragged down by the panicked, drowning man.

To Eliza's welcome surprise, the victim of the mires was not at all heavy and she was able to pull the figure out onto the banks with relative ease. It was only when he was halfway out of the water, coughing and spluttering for breath that she realised it was a boy near her own age. Realising this, Eliza worked all the harder to help the lad onto the shore, sacrificing her footing a little now she knew the boy's weight wouldn't threaten to drag her down into the water with him.

As the boy opened his eyes and took in much-needed lungsful of air, he seemed to become better aware of his surroundings, working with Eliza as he engaged his hands and knees and crawled onto the shore. At last, he was on dry land. He rolled onto his back, staring up into the sky and panting profusely as his mind processed the near-death experience.

"Are you all right? What happened to you? What are you doing out here on your own? Do you have a name?"

Eliza was a whirlwind of questions as she leaned over the boy, eyes wide with fright as she looked him over for injury.

"I'm... fine," the boy assured, between much-needed gasps of air. "I am so grateful for you coming when you did. I didn't know anyone else was out here." He looked to Eliza, flashing a warm bright smile. His immaculate, white teeth contrasted with the dark mud that covered his face and drew a little giggle from Eliza. She had to hand it to the boy, he was remarkably calm and cheerful for having almost drowned.

"What's your name?" Eliza asked again.

"Oh, I'm sorry. Stanford at your service, Edward Stanford."

Eliza's eyes widened, and her mouth opened ever so slightly as she tried to comprehend just what she was hearing. "Stanford... You mean... you're the Earl's son?"

"Younger son," Edward said sounding almost defensive.

"Well, what are you doing out here on the fens?" Eliza asked, her mind-boggling as she tried to contrive some reason for someone of rank to be trudging through the mud like a common leech collector.

"I was looking for a toad," Edward answered, his look seeming to suggest that this was all the explanation that was needed.

Eliza shook her head, thoroughly bewildered. Her father had often said that very rich people were prone to strange habits and hobbies, but she had never expected anything like this. She resisted the urge to ask further questions regarding the boy's business, though, focusing her mind as she noticed his whole body begin to shiver.

"Your clothes are soaked through, and the water is freezing," she said, shrugging off her own overcoat and wrapping it around the boy. "We need to get you indoors and by a fire quickly or you could catch a chill or worse."

Edward, nodded, his teeth beginning to chatter manically as the adrenaline of his fall and rescue wore off. Suddenly he became acutely aware of how cold he truly was, unable to feel any of his extremities as the girl threw her coat about him. "What about you," Edward asked, looking to Eliza's bare shoulders and thin clothes. "You'll be freezing."

"I haven't taken a dip in the bog," Eliza reminded, forcing her coat about the Earl's son and making sure it would not fall. Edward was a little taller than her and the coat did not exactly fit him, but it had to serve. "Can you walk? I can lead you back to my house, and mother will take care of you."

Edward looked about in the mists, peering through the gloom. "You... you know the way back to the village through this?"

"I've been working out here for years," Eliza explained as she helped the boy to his feet, wrapping an arm about him to keep him steady and offer further warmth. "If you stick with me, I can get you back to civilisation, and hopefully without any further accidents."

Edward nodded, shuffling forward across the firmer bank as Eliza began to lead him carefully through the mists.

"What's your name?" Edward asked after they had walked a little way together.

"Eliza, Eliza Thorn."

"Good name," Edward said with a nod, suppressing another shudder that wracked his body. "Why are you out here?"

"I'm collecting leeches to bring to the doctor," Eliza said. "Let's hope you don't catch a fever from being out here and need any yourself."

"I hate leeches," Edward confirmed, his face bunching up a little. "Do you need to collect your things before we go back?"

"Honestly, I'm more worried about getting you to a fire before your joints freeze up like a statue," Eliza replied.

"Please, you've done so much for me already. If you need to collect anything, I would want you to do so before we turn back. I wouldn't feel right knowing I've cost you a day's work."

Eliza felt the young boy's priorities were horribly out of kilter, but she could not help but smile. She had not thought the Stanfords could be so polite. They were never seen in the village at all except when the Lord's carriage charged through the streets.

To alleviate Edward's concerns and owing to it being on the way back anyway, Eliza did retrieve her bag and the three jars of torpid leeches she had collected for the doctor. After that, she and the young boy had a long and ponderous journey through the mists to get back to the village. Had she been alone, Eliza might have completed the journey in under an hour. Edward, however, slowed her immeasurably. His steps were slow, and he struggled to make the jumps between the patches of dry earth that dotted the fens. He was stiff, and the cold was clearly affecting him more than he let on. At all times he told Eliza not to worry, but moment by moment she feared what would become of the boy. Eliza had heard of people dying from a fall in the icy waters on a cold winter's day. Dreadful fevers could set in, and some simply died before they could be brought to a warm fire. She did not look to frighten Edward by sharing her fears, just prayed silently that they would make it back to the village and her father's home in time.

After an incalculable time struggling through the mists of the swamp, Eliza and Edward finally made it onto the firmer, solid ground of the fields that bordered the village of Denton. Eliza had hoped their going would be smoother after that, but every step they took seemed to grow slower and slower as Edward seemed to grow weary and drowsy by her side. Eliza panicked, her own body stiffening in fright as she watched the boy's eyes close down.

"Hey, stay awake now; it's not time for bed," Eliza admonished, trying to keep her tone light and airy even as fear gripped her.

"I'm not falling asleep," Edward returned, sounding a little insulted. Even for his reply, his eyes remained heavy-lidded and his steps stumbling. He looked more and more like he was on the verge of collapse, and Eliza wracked her brain to think of any subject that might keep him alert, keep him with her. It was as she looked out to the distant town, seeing lights piercing the mists, that an idea came to her.

"I imagine Christmas on the Stanford estate must be something to behold. Your family only ever comes here for the holiday season, it seems."

"We come... come here other times," Edward replied, his words a mumble as his head hung limp and Eliza had to put more effort into keeping him propped up.

"What's Christmas like on your estate, what do you eat?" Eliza's voice was rapidly becoming panicked, unable to disguise the fright in her voice anymore as she tried to keep the boy with her.

"We normally eat goose," Edward said. "You should come and eat with us."

"Eat with you?" Eliza looked to Edward, feeling as though the boy's mumbles were turning to incoherency to hear so foolish a suggestion. "I don't think I'm the kind of guest you want around your Christmas table, My Lord."

"I'm not a Lord," Edward replied, his voice becoming suddenly firmer and his eyes opening a fraction further. "Martin, he's the one set to be the Earl."

"Well, I think you'd make a fine Lord," Eliza said, now resorting to saying the first thing that came into her head.

"I couldn't be a Lord. I couldn't even find a toad to take home to show my brother how capable I am."

"Well, I am sure when we get you to my home I can go back out onto the marshes and find you a toad. In fact, I guarantee it. Just keep walking with me and I'll get you all the toads you could ever want."

"No… need to do it myself," Edward continued to mumble. "You should still come to dinner though. Least I can do to thank you for… for…"

Eliza shook Edward then, pressing her body even closer to the boy to lend him her warmth. "Hey, come on now.

Focus. Tell me more about this dinner. I'm not partial to goose. Anything else you can give me?"

To Eliza's relief, Edward retained his faculties just long enough for them to reach the road that led to the village. He did not hold out beyond that, crumpling into her arms and forcing her to lay him down by the bushes. They had come far enough though. Civilisation was close, and she hollered loudly and desperately down the way, waving to the shadows she could see passing through the village beyond. The snow was just beginning to fall, the sky darkening and a sudden flurry coming down hard. She left Edward in the grass, snowflakes peppering his muddied clothes and skin as she ran down the way screaming as though she had robbers at her heels.

"Hey! Help! Help!"

Her head turned and, at last, Eliza was seen. She felt relief wash through her as the local smith and the local innkeeper abandoned their work and followed her out down the road. Eliza was too overwhelmed with emotion to explain anything coherently at that moment. She could only lead the men over to Edward's unconscious form, pointing dumbly down at his pale, frozen body. His skin had almost the same colour as the snow that rested on his chest and both men gave worried looks to one another.

"I found him in the marshes," Eliza managed to say at last. "He fell in the water, and I pulled him out."

The smith leaned down and picked the boy up as though he weighed no more than a fallen twig. Throwing Edward over his back he looked to the innkeeper.

"We'll get him in by the fire. Eliza, go fetch the doctor at once. Do you know who the boy is, who are his parents?"

"He's Lord Stanford's son," Eliza said, noting the disbelief in the two men as their fears grew all the more.

"What's the Lord's boy doing traipsing through the marshes?" The smith and innkeeper gave confused looks to one another but recovered quickly. The smith jogged down the lane quickly, Edward bouncing on his shoulder as he went. Other villagers were stopping to look and stare at the unusual sight, many of the women gasping and muttering to themselves as they watched the man rush to the inn at speed.

"Get to the Doctor at once," the innkeeper shouted to Eliza as he followed behind.

Eager to be of any assistance, Eliza did as she was told, rushing past the small gaggle of gawkers who had stopped to stare.

Evening had fallen over the village by the time Lord Stanford's carriage pulled up in the village. The Earl's black carriage had always seemed somewhat intimidating to Eliza. Its obsidian black paint always felt ominous to her, and the speed at which the equally black stallions rushed through the village was enough to scare any villager walking. There had never been any accidents, but many feared being trampled under hooves and wheels every time that carriage passed through town.

Eliza had lingered by Edward's side throughout the day, or at least stayed put on the ground floor of the inn while the boy was tended to upstairs in the best room the inn had to offer. A few suggested she was in the way, that she had done all she could to help the boy. They reminded her that chores were waiting for her at home, but none of these concerns persuaded Eliza to leave her post, watching over the young man she had rescued. The adults around her seemed subtly aware of this and, after a time, gave up on telling her what to do and merely asked that she stay out of the way if she insisted on lingering.

A flurry of snow rushed in through the door, causing the fire in the hearth to flicker and a chill to run straight through Eliza's body. She looked to the figure in the doorway recognising the man by the cut of his clothes alone. She had to be looking at the Earl of Stanford, George Grisham. He was a tall man, his height accentuated by the hat he wore. It was a tall stovepipe hat. His billowing coat made him almost formless as he stood in the doorway. The only colour to the man, at all, came from the flash of silver that crowned his cane. His gloved hands obscured much of that round, silver pommel, but it still stood out against the black thread that made up the rest of him.

Stepping into the inn, the Earl did not think to close the door behind him. The innkeeper's daughter, a girl of fifteen, had to rush across the room to do it, while the Earl took off his hat and brushed snow from the brim.

Lost in worry and concern for Edward, Eliza hadn't paid much attention to the weather outside. She had been vaguely aware that the snow had kept up all through the afternoon, but it was only now as she saw the thick white powder on the earl that she realised how bad the weather had turned. She was all the more thankful she and Edward had managed to find civilisation when they had. If they had been caught in the snow, who knew if either of them could have made it back to the village in one piece.

"You there, do you work here? Where is my son?" The Earl's voice was a sharp bark, and his orders demanded a quick answer. On instinct, Eliza rose to her feet, straightening up like a soldier on parade.

"I don't work here, M'lord, but your son is upstairs with the doctor. He hasn't left Edward... I mean your son's side, since he came in."

Eliza bit her bottom lip, colour rising to her cheeks in embarrassment at referring to the Lord's son so informally. The Earl had certainly picked up on it by the way his eyes seemed to narrow, and his lip curled in frustration. He was the sort of man who could easily inspire terror in others. Aside from his height and his imposing clothes, he had eyes the colour of flint and his sharp angular features were just as stony. Eliza lowered her gaze in apology, wringing her hands together as she stared down at her feet. To her relief, the man's concern for his son won out over any insult or frustration she had caused. The Lord stalked across the floor of the inn. He moved up the stairs without an introduction to the lady of the house or the innkeeper, acting as though he owned the place. And maybe he did. Everything in the village was on the Earl's land and nearly all the families were tenants of his.

Eliza waited for a few minutes before she allowed herself to move again. She stayed where she was in the corner of the bottom floor, waiting cautiously and alertly lest the Lord return. When he did not, she moved over to the stairs and gave a curious glance to the upper floors.

"You really should think of going home soon," the innkeeper's daughter suggested as she moved toward the kitchens. "Anyone will think you're fishing for some kind of reward for having found the Lord's son if you keep lingering like that. It's unseemly."

"I don't want a reward, I just want to know he is well," Eliza answered. Still, she moved away from the stairs then, remembering again that she should not get in the way of the doctor or any others who might need to pass by.

"You aren't going to be told anything," the innkeeper's girl said, very matter-of-factly. "The boy's health is none of your business really. I shouldn't wonder if the Earl will have him put straight in his carriage and the doctor brought up to their estate. After that, we probably won't hear anything more of it. If he dies, I'm sure it'll make the papers and you can find out about it then."

Eliza did not find the girl's words at all reassuring. Once again, she ignored the suggested course to leave and moved back to the corner where she took a seat.

Minutes passed. From time to time, Eliza could hear mumblings and footsteps from upstairs but nothing substantial. Her first clue to Edward's health came when the boy was carried down the stairs in the innkeeper's arms, wrapped up in blankets and pale as the grave. His father followed behind, along with the doctor at the rear. The three men stopped to look to Eliza, Edward weakly pointing in her direction. "She's the one, father."

Eliza stiffened as, once again, the Earl shot her a glance that was far from hospitable. She wondered what Edward could possibly have said to the man but wouldn't dare to ask.

"It might do the boy good to have her near if it will sooth him," the doctor said, his voice quiet and humble. Eliza did not know what was going on and looked between the three men with a knotted brow.

"You have family nearby?" the Earl asked, his voice still clipped and aggressive.

"Just down the road from here," Eliza answered, pointing dumbly in the vague direction of home.

"I can go to the girl's parents if it pleases you, M'Lord," the innkeeper piped up. "They have already been informed she is here, and I am sure will have no objections if they know the request came from you."

The earl gave a kind of grunt in acknowledgement as he put his hat on, taking time and care to ensure it was affixed in just the proper way to his head. "Very well then. You are to come with me, child."

"With you?" Eliza looked to the Earl, every fibre of her being wanting to be as far away from the grim and scary-looking man as she could. But the sight of Edward in the innkeeper's arms gave her pause. She wanted to know the boy was well, did not want her only word on his health to come from the papers.

Looking back to the earl, she wondered if she was even allowed to refuse someone so important. If he told her to follow him, she surely had only one answer.

"Come on, child. I don't have all day, and neither does my son," the Earl growled, turning away from Eliza and pushing for the door. The doctor, a man who Eliza had known for years through her work, came to her side and ushered her along.

"Don't worry, Eliza. The Earl is just worried for his son, and I think the lad will benefit from having you nearby. It might be some delirium, but he called for you several times as he stirred in and out of consciousness."

"He called for me?" Despite the gravity of the situation, Eliza could not help but feel a certain importance at having been on the boy's heart and mind as he slipped in and out of sleep.

"You'll come with us to the Earl's manor and can assist me where needed," the doctor continued. "You know your way around my medicine bag well enough after so many years. Make yourself useful and, when needed, you can keep the young Lord company. It'll be your job to keep him calm and centred."

"Calm and centred," Eliza repeated, taking a deep breath and stealing herself for the task ahead. She did not know how much good her presence would do, but if it would help Edward recover, then she was going to do all within her power to help him.

CHAPTER 3

Eliza had only ever seen Lord Stanford's home from far away. It was a grand Manor House that sat atop a large hill overlooking the surrounding countryside. A river divided the manor from the roadways on one side, and the wetlands stretched far to the east and south of the property. Only one road led up to the estate, meaning that, unless there was cause for a person to visit, no one from the village ever needed to go near the place. Eliza had understood that a few brave souls from the village occasionally snuck onto the Earl's lands at night, poaching from the Earl's lake, but beyond this, the man's home felt like another world, as distant from the village of Denton as the pearly gates of heaven. Now, she was passing down the main drive of the property, peering out the window at the trees and grounds. In the winter's dark, with the moon obscured behind the blackened snow clouds, she could not make out much. But certain shadows that passed by gave the suggestion of ornamental fountains or of expertly cut hedges trimmed to symmetrical shapes. The most striking view, and the only thing she could see clearly from the carriage window, was the light streaming in from the windows of the manor.

The whole place shone like a beacon in the night, and Eliza was reminded once again of the seasonal holiday, as each window reminded her of the candles lit in the parish church on Christmas Day. It was a silly thought though, and she banished it quickly from her mind when she realised the earl was once again studying her closely with that worrisome expression that caused her to tremble.

"Well, here we are," the Earl said as the carriage trundled to a halt at the front of the property. "My men will bring Edward inside, Doctor. You and the girl are to wait in the entryway and will be escorted up to his chambers when he is settled in bed." The Earl paused and looked to Eliza. "I don't much care for the child's presence here and trust she will truly make herself useful?"

"She seems to give your son comfort, M'lord," the doctor replied. "Given the uncertainty of his condition and his somewhat confused state of mind, it would be a sensible precaution to make use of anything that might aid him in coming back to himself."

The Earl gave another grunt by way of reply. It seemed to be his way when forced to acquiesce to something altogether against his own will. "Just make sure the girl is supervised at all times. I do not want her wandering the corridors like a vagrant."

"I assure you, when she is not looking after your son directly, she will be helping me with my things," the doctor replied.

The carriage door opened and all within the vehicle flinched as another blast of cold winter's air assailed them. Eliza looked to Edward, the only one who seemed untroubled by the icy tumult that circulated the carriage. She did not take his quiet as a good sign and watched with mounting concern as the footman reached in and bundled the lad into his arms.

"Take him straight up to his chambers and have the doctor and this girl taken to him when ready," the earl snapped. "And take care that Lady Stanford does not see the state of him. She was hysterical enough when she realised that he was missing this morning."

"Yes, M'Lord," the footman said with a gracious bow.

On instinct, Eliza moved to rise from her seat, to follow Edward. Doctor Horner, however, put out a hand to bar her way, casting her a stern glance. They had to wait for the earl to rise and leave the carriage first. Such protocol and politeness seemed a little unnecessary to Eliza at that moment when Edward's life seemed to hang in the balance, still, she did not move to object. She watched as the Earl rose from his seat, helped down by another servant who followed him up the stone steps to the front door of the property. Both Eliza and the doctor were left almost to fend for themselves. A servant did come over to take Doctor Horner's medicine bag, but otherwise, they received no assistance at all as they trudged through the ankle-deep snow to the front door.

Though she knew her thoughts should be centred on Edward, Eliza could not help but pause as she stepped through the front doors of the manor into the Earl's home. There was much to catch her attention. The vibrant red of the carpet that lined the entryway and ran all the way to the grand stairwell that led to the second floor, the chandelier above her made of crystal that seemed so heavy that Eliza feared it might fall and crush her at any moment. Still, what struck Eliza the most as she stepped into the hallway was the light. The hall was lit as though it was the middle of the day in the height of summer. It was truly breath taking, and Eliza could not even count the number of candles and lights that helped suffuse the room with such a warm and inviting glow. The doctor seemed less impressed by the grandeur of the place. As Eliza came to an awed stop in the entryway, he put a hand to her back and steered her onward, reminding her again of the need to follow the Earl's orders exactly and not make a nuisance of herself.

Letting Doctor Horner guide her way, Eliza found herself led to the side of the main door. Servants came to take their coats, one giving Eliza a questioning, almost insulting look as he took in the ragged, muddy mess of her clothes. The way he turned his nose up at her caused Eliza to blush. A mix of embarrassment and frustration filled her, and she wished the Earl had not invited her at all if he and his household took such objection to her. Still, she was here for Edward. Reminding herself of that fact allowed her to face the servant's incredulous look with a new defiance.

~

For a time, Eliza and the doctor were left by the door, made to stand about almost as though they were part of the furniture. Determined to prove she would not be any trouble for Doctor Horner, Eliza remained quiet the whole time, eyes darting this way and that as she took in the opulence before her. Several paintings lined the walls, including a portrait of the Earl and his wife that dominated the centre of the grand stairwell. Eliza took it all in and felt without exaggeration that the hall in which she stood must be worth more on its own than the entire village of Denton.

As her eyes studied the exquisite floral carving on the bannister rails of the stairwell, Eliza thought she heard something from the corridor above. She glanced up, seeing a head poking out from over the bannister and looking down at her with interest. This boy, Eliza was sure, had to be Edward's older brother.

The lad was taller than Edward, probably twelve or thirteen years of age, Eliza guessed. He had short hair, cut in a very severe fashion. It must have been blonde once, but age was seeing the golden strands turn to a darker brown. He had his father's angular features, a sharp nose like a crow's beak and sallow cheeks. He was by no means as intimidating as his father, but the youth was the very picture of what Eliza imagined a Lord to be—proud, snobbish, and aloof. He looked down at Eliza, lips smirking as though finding her presence in his home subtly amusing. He put his hands behind his back and walked slowly down the steps, eyes on Eliza the entire time.

"So, it's true, my idiot brother did find a vagrant out in the swamp. What business do you have foraging in the muck, girl? Your family send you out hunting for frogs and rats to feed your brothers and sisters? Eliza's face bunched up, disgusted at the idea that the boy could live in such a fashion. She did not dare to correct him though, knowing full well the kind of scolding she'd receive if she dared talk back to her betters in such a way.

"I asked you a question, girl," the boy spoke, his voice darkening and causing Eliza to flinch a little as he drew closer.

"She works for me, young Master," Doctor Horner interjected, coming to Eliza's rescue. "The medicinal leeches used to drain bad blood and correct the humours are found in the wetlands. Miss Thorn here does a very useful job in collecting them for me and I, in turn, send on those I don't need to other doctors in London to help treat the sick."

Eliza straightened up a little, feeling just a small glow of pride at the Doctor's explanation.

"Sounds like a horrible, disgusting job. I bet your legs are a mess of love bites from those nasty little bloodsuckers."

Eliza's lips drew thin, and she resolved to ignore the comment. She wished Edward's brother would leave her alone, ignore her as his father and the other servants seemed to do. But, for whatever reason, the boy was determined to engage her, prowling about her like some predator teasing a trapped fawn.

"I can certainly see what my brother sees in you," the boy continued. "Edward has never had much luck fitting in amongst his class. Then again, it is so hard for a second son to be counted an equal in our set. It must be nice for him to have made a friend who might be impressed by him just because he lives in a fancy house and wears fine clothes."

Eliza squirmed where she stood, feeling a need to answer the boy, and knowing to do such a thing would only invite rebuke and censure upon herself. Fortunately, she was saved for a second time as the Earl's ominous voice boomed from the upstairs. "Martin, do not go teasing the young woman. A man of class and substance never looks to show off to a girl so far beneath him. Do you tease ants in the gardens for being bigger than them?"

"No father, what would be the point?" Martin asked, clearly not understanding the metaphor.

"Go to your mother, now. I do not want her left on her own fretting for too long. It is bad enough Edward is at death's door. The last thing I want to see is your mother getting another of her awful headaches."

Eliza looked to Martin, the youth sucking in a breath through gritted teeth as he nodded and went on his way. It seemed, for all his bravado, he knew who truly ruled the roost in the manor and was as subservient as any other when the Earl spoke.

Lord Stanford watched his son depart, eyes not leaving the boy until he was finally out of the room.

"I did not intend to play messenger, but I have it on good authority that everything is set up for you in Edward's room," the Earl said. "You may go on up to him now. I do not want you being any further distraction for my son."

The Earl drifted away, disappearing from view before the Doctor could even answer, and he and Eliza were forced to move quickly up the stairs after the man. As they went, Eliza had to wonder about the family Edward was born into. Both Edward's father and his older brother seemed so completely different in temperament from Edward that Eliza could scarce believe they were at all related. Though she knew Edward would likely be unconscious in his room, Eliza was sure she would feel more welcomed and at home at his sickbed than she would be anywhere else in the house. Stanford Manor, though grand and opulent, seemed very dark and inhospitable to her indeed.

∽

Brought to Edward's room, the Earl quickly made his excuses to leave, entrusting his son to Doctor Horner's care. Yet again, Eliza noticed the Earl's casual indifference as he wandered off, not seeming at all troubled by the idea that his youngest son might be lingering on the precipice between life and death. Then again, it was possible the man just wished to save face, hiding his true feelings for fear of showing weakness. Eliza certainly hoped this was the case.

Stepping into Edward's bedroom, Eliza was once again struck by how grand a world her new friend belonged to if 'friends' was indeed the right word for what she and Edward were. His room had its very own fireplace, the hearth bigger than the one in Eliza's own living room and kitchen back in the village. There was a generous, roaring fire already lit, casting bright light in the bedroom. It was enough for Eliza to wonder if Edward and his family really knew what darkness was at all, or whether they lived in perpetual daylight in their grand Manor House.

"How is he?" Eliza asked, shaking off her awe and focusing on Edward who lay in the bed under crisp, white sheets.

"It is too early to say," Doctor Horner answered. "He has a much better chance than many in his condition, but lingering for hours out in the cold after taking a tumble into frozen water... there are no guarantees."

Eliza moved over to Edward's side, her brow knotting in worry and tears blurring her vision ever so slightly as she looked down at the boy. His face and body had been cleaned since she last saw him. It was strange for Eliza to think that this was the first time she had truly seen him, getting a true look at his features.

Edward did not look even the shade of his father or brother. His face was rounder, softer. His hair was cut short, just as Martin's had been, but Edward had blonde, radiant hair that shone like gold filigree as the firelight illuminated his features. His skin was white, deathly so, and if it weren't for the slight rise and fall of his chest beneath the sheets, Eliza would have sworn she was looking down at a corpse. She pressed forward, hands moving to settle on the sheets.

"Ah, Eliza, do not lean on the bed like that. Your hands are no doubt grubby, and I do not want the Earl complaining that you have left stains on the boy's bed."

"Oh... um, I am sorry, doctor," Eliza said, drawing back and putting her hands behind her back.

"There's a basin just over there. Wash up good and proper and then I'll inspect your hands," the man said, his voice kind and gentle despite his sharp order.

Eliza did everything Dr Horner told her. She washed her hands in the basin, pleased to find the water warm to the touch. She scrubbed under her nails and splashed her face, taking advantage of the dressing mirror to make sure every fleck of dirt and mud was off her body before rejoining the doctor at Edward's side. Even after so many precautions, she still felt uneasy putting her hands on anything in the boy's quarters but she seemed to have done enough to placate her employer, and he soon set her to work checking the young man's temperature, applying hot towels to his forehead and counting the beats of his pulse from time to time.

All through her work, Eliza hounded the doctor with questions. Though his answers rarely seemed to change, Eliza could not help herself. Every time she placed another hot towel on Edward's head, every time she checked his pulse, she always asked the question in case her last duty had been the one to cure him of his ills.

The doctor was quick to put to work the leeches Eliza had brought from the fens that morning. The little black, jewelled worms collected in her jars had been roused to new life by the warmth of the young man's bedroom and Doctor Horner was quick to apply them to the boy's arm to draw out any bad blood. Eliza watched as each one grew fat on the boy's blood, pulling each away and helping the doctor replace them as needed. It was a grim job and Eliza did not like to see the creatures feasting on her new friend in such a way, but it was all for his benefit, she knew.

The hours drew on and after drawing out as much blood as he deemed necessary, the doctor ordered Eliza to remove the leeches from Edward's arm while he fell asleep in a chair. A clock on the mantelpiece told Eliza it was half one in the morning, but she did not feel at all sleepy as she kept her firm and determined vigil over Edward. He was her duty and responsibility. She had saved him from drowning in the fens and she would do everything within her power to ensure her work and effort was not in vain.

Watching the clock draw closer to two o'clock, Eliza wondered if she should perhaps change the towel on Edward's head again. She did not wish to wake the doctor to ask him and decided it could only be a good thing. She gently lifted the cooling towel from Edward's forehead when she noticed him move beneath the sheets, the first time he had stirred since their arrival.

"Edward?" she whispered his name, eyes lighting with hope and body tensing as she leaned over him and watched his eyes. She could see his eyelids fluttering ever so slightly and Eliza's excitement mounted as she noticed his lips tremble.

"Eliza…"

He spoke. Eliza felt excitement and relief, not to mention as certain pride rushed through her at the boy's first word. She had found it hard to believe the boy had truly been asking for her back at the inn, and it touched her heart to be the first word formed on his lips as he regained consciousness. Eliza knew she should probably wake the doctor, but she was glued to Edward's side, reaching out to take his hand and squeezing it comfortingly.

"I'm here Edward, it's me. We made it! We made it to the village." Eliza's words were an urgent whisper and she continued to study the boy's every slight movement as his eyes slowly fluttered open and he turned his head to look at her.

"We made it?" he asked, the question spoken in such a way as to suggest he had completely forgotten where they were going in the first place. "Where are we?"

"Don't… don't you even recognise your own room?" Eliza asked, her own brow creasing with new worry as it seemed his mind was not as together as she had hoped.

"My room?" Edward looked about him and drew in a breath. There was a suggestion of recollection on his face as he took in the fireplace, the chest of draws, the wardrobe. "How did we get here? Are you here for Christmas?"

"Yes, yes, I am here for Christmas." Eliza giggled, surprised the boy could remember that odd snippet of conversation spoken when he was on the verge of collapse. "You invited me here, remember?"

"I remember," Edward said, trying to push up a little in bed but his limbs failing him.

"Oh, easy there," Eliza soothed. "You've been asleep for hours now and the doctor took quite a lot of blood from you. It's probably best you lie still."

"Probably best," Edward agreed, settling his head back into the pillows. There was a moment's pause, Eliza wondering again if she should wake the doctor but also wishing to just enjoy this moment with Edward. She felt curiously bound to him, perhaps because of their shared ordeal in the fens. She pursed her lips, a question rising to her mind as she considered something he had said when they had first met.

"Edward... did you tell me your brother dared you to go out into the wetlands and find that toad you were looking for?"

"Yes," Edward answered, his voice hoarse and rasping.

Eliza grabbed the water jug and filled a glass which she brought to the boy's lips. "I know it is not my business to tell you what to do, but I don't think you should listen to your brother's dares in the future. I... I don't think he has your best interests at heart." Eliza felt a slight tingle of fear as she spoke, knowing it was not right or proper to set Edward against his brother or to speak ill of the boy who was one day to become an earl. Still, she could not help but share her fear.

"I won't be going out into the fens again, at least not without you as a guide," Edward replied between grateful sips of water. For the time being, this was enough for Eliza, and she felt once again that sensation of warmth at the thought that Edward would put such trust in her or even want to go out with her on the marshes again. Strangely, the idea seemed quite pleasant to her, absurd though the notion was.

Carried away by her thoughts, Eliza didn't pay enough attention as she held the water glass. Accidentally forcing too much on the boy at once, Edward coughed and spluttered, the sound startling Dr Horner awake.

"Goodness, you're awake! Eliza, you should have told me at once."

"It was my fault, doctor," Edward jumped in immediately, his attempt to shield Eliza from admonishment falling on deaf ears as the doctor immediately looked to check over the boy and run some tests. Eliza stepped back, noticing the way Edward's eyes continually glanced her way as the doctor did his work. Though she had been reminded several times there were no guarantees when it came to Edward's health, Eliza could not help but feel all was going to be well for him now. With bed rest and care, he would be back to full strength and life in no time. Then, she realised, she would have to return to the village, and they would likely never see one another again.

CHAPTER 4

It was early the next morning before Edward was allowed any visitors in his room beyond Dr Horner and Eliza. It struck Eliza as strange and a little sad that neither the boy's father nor brother came to call on him. It showcased for her again the strange distance she had felt between the family members the previous evening, and her heart went out to Edward for being trapped in such an apparently loveless home. However, when at last the doctor deemed Edward strong enough to receive visitors, Eliza was pleased to find one member of his family had made the effort.

If Lord Stanford was the moon, then Lady Stanford was the sun. On her very first glimpse of the lady of the house, Eliza realised Edward's mother was quite different from the earl and no doubt it was from her that Edward had inherited both his softer looks and his more pleasing temperament. As soon as she was permitted to enter, Lady

Stanford swept into the room, her skirts ruffling as she rushed across the room and practically jumped onto the bed and embraced her son.

"Oh Edward, we were so worried about you. How... how could you put me through this again. Are you actually trying to break my heart and kill me!" Though her words were all rebuke, Eliza could hear the gratitude and relief in Lady Stanford's voice as she hugged and kissed her boy. It was a warming sight and left Eliza feeling a little more at peace with Edward's lot.

"What on earth happened, why did you go out into the fens all by yourself like that?" The woman, at last, drew back from Edward, flicking strands of her own golden, blonde hair from her face as she fixed her son with a stern expression.

"It was Martin. He told me I had to go out into the fens and find a toad to prove I could handle myself and be a man. He said—"

"—That's a lie, you little worm!"

Eliza jumped at the interruption, her body tensing as Martin flew into the room, his hands balled into fists and an angry glint in his eye as he marched toward Edward's bed. "He's just trying to make a fool of you again, mother. He told me he was going on an expedition into the marshes, and I merely told him I didn't believe him. When he said he'd come back with a toad to prove it to me, I said I didn't care and told him he was being irresponsible even to risk himself in such a way."

Eliza drew in a deep breath, puffing up in indignation. Though she had no right to judge, she felt with absolute certainty that Martin was lying, looking to cover his own back now his brother had returned. His callousness shocked her, especially when the dare he had sent Edward on had almost resulted in his death. Eliza hardly wished to believe it, but she almost wondered if Martin wanted that. At the very least, he had seemed quite at peace with the notion of being left an only child when she had seen him the previous night.

"Now, Martin, mind yourself," Lady Stanford said, putting out a hand to stop Martin from getting anywhere near Edward. "Your brother is still very ill, and I am sure is not in the right state of mind presently. I am sure your father will get to the bottom of what happened yesterday in due course, but I will not have you agitating your brother's condition by arguing or fighting with him again."

Eliza raised a brow at that last word, her concern for Edward mounting yet again as she looked to Martin.

"I have no doubt Father will have you sent to that school like he has been threatening to, these last eight years," Martin jeered, getting in one last jibe before his mother pointed to the door.

"That is enough, Martin, on your way, or I will tell your father that you both need punishing for this whole fiasco."

It was hard for Eliza not to smile at that moment. She knew it was not right and she certainly did not wish Edward's dark-tempered older brother seeing her enjoy his scolding, but she could hardly help it. To mask her satisfaction, she turned about and made a show of straightening out the towels she had been interchanging and placing on Edward's forehead. Though her back was turned, she was sure Martin saw her. She could feel his gaze, hateful and mean, on her and she stiffened a little as she waited for that foreboding feeling to leave her.

"On your way now," Lady Stanford said again, her words accompanied this time with a slamming of the door as Martin, at last, followed orders. Eliza turned back around, looking to Edward with some concern.

"You know you really shouldn't wind your brother up like that," Lady Stanford chided, her voice far gentler as she berated her youngest son. "You know how he gets, and you should know your quarrels never end well for you."

"But mother, Martin really did tell me to go out onto the marshes! I'm not saying it to get him into trouble. It's just what happened."

Lady Stanford pursed her lips and sucked in a breath. "You know, maybe it would be for the best for you to be sent away for your education... As much as it pains me to admit it, neither of you do well around one another. Martin brings out the little scoundrel in you and you are constantly feeling his temper..." The woman trailed off, an unhappy look on her face as she considered the options before her son. Eliza could tell the lady had a deep love for her boys, both of them, and she was loath to send either one away.

Perhaps looking to clear the air or avoid the darker subjects that brought her so much misery and unhappiness, Lady Stanford turned to look at Eliza, her smile returning as she studied her.

"So, this must be the little 'lady of the lake' who helped you come back to shore."

Edward sat up a little, nodding enthusiastically. "This is Eliza Thorn. I don't know what you've been told by father, but I'd most certainly be dead if it weren't for her."

"Really?" Lady Stanford's voice suggested a certain apprehension and Eliza guessed the woman had not been informed of Edward's true condition by the Earl.

"It's the truth, mother, and we have to do something to thank her," Edward continued, a look of resolve on his face as he looked to his mother. "I promised her she could stay for Christmas."

Lady Stanford looked to her son in surprise, discomfort spreading across her features as she looked back at Eliza. She laughed, almost seeming to hope Edward might call the whole thing a practical joke. But his serious, earnest expression remained.

"Edward, you can't just invite strangers to dinner, no matter what they may be or what they have done for you. It is your father who says who can and can't dine with us and I am sure Miss Thorn here would not wish to be embarrassed by dining with others so far above her station and class."

Eliza bit her bottom lip. She had originally been quite attracted by the prospect of sharing a Christmas meal with Edward and his family, but this was before she had met the boy's father and brother. Both left her feeling frightened and entirely unwelcome in the home and the last thing Eliza wanted was to sit down with them to share a meal.

"It is honestly no trouble at all, your ladyship," Eliza piped up with a polite curtsey. "I do not need any thanks for what I did. I am sure any other soul who saw your son struggling in the mire would have done the same."

"But mother, we can't just send her home with nought but a thank you," Edward protested. Even with Eliza assuring him that all was well, the boy seemed adamant that she be given some kind of reward for all she had done.

Lady Stanford looked between Eliza and Edward, her lips pursed thin and brows knitted close together as she seemed to try to wrap her head around the conundrum set for her. "I agree it would be less than Christian for us to do nothing for the girl as thanks for delivering you home safely... What is it you do, little girl?"

"I am a leech collector," Eliza said, staring down at her feet as her cheeks flushed with embarrassment. It felt silly saying such a thing when standing in so grand a house and in such noble company. Just admitting to her profession was a painful reminder that she had really no business being there at all.

"I see," Lady Stanford said, her own expression hardening a little. "Tell me, do you do chores at home to help your mother?"

"I wash up, cook a little, sew and knit and sweep..." Eliza began to list all the things she would do when her morning on the marshes was complete, pausing at times to consider any other talents she put to use for her mother.

"Well, perhaps I can do one thing to thank your friend for all she has done for you," Lady Stanford said with a smile.

"Really, what is it?" Edward asked, eagerly looking to his mother for an explanation.

"The cook has been on at me for some time about hiring some more help in the kitchens, and as I am in charge of the housekeeping, it is on my say-so who is brought in to fill that role," Lady Stanford began.

Eliza felt a tremble run through her before Lady Stanford was even done talking. She could easily guess at the woman's next words even if she could not quite believe them. She stared dumbfounded at Edward's mother, the lady smiling warmly back at her. "The work will be hard and there will be a steep learning curve for you if you are to thrive and do well. However, starting off in the kitchens will mean that you cannot get into too much trouble and should be trained properly so long as you are diligent and attentive."

"You mean you wish to have Eliza wash our dishes?" Edward asked, his voice suggesting surprise and a little frustration. "Mother, I want to thank Eliza for rescuing me from the bogs not give her chores to do about the house."

Eliza stepped forward, quickly holding up her hands and shaking her head at Edward as a sign for him to be quiet. "Please, I would be very happy to accept such a position within your household." She spoke swiftly, eager to prevent Edward from trying to change his mother's mind. "You do not know what such a thing would mean to me, and I promise I will prove myself with any task you choose to give me."

"Really, this is truly something you want?" Edward asked, turning to Eliza and looking somewhat surprised. Eliza could guess the boy had no idea of what such a position would mean for her and her family's fortunes. Edward likely hadn't had to worry once about money in his life.

"Believe me, my little scamp, Miss Eliza should find things far more agreeable in our kitchens, scrubbing dishes, than traipsing through the fens looking for blood-sucking leeches. Don't you think that would be a far better job for her?"

"I suppose so," Edward said. He still did not appear altogether happy but his face lighted as a thought struck. "I suppose if you were to come and work here in the manor, I could come and see you whenever I wish."

"Well, that would certainly be nice of you, but remember Eliza would be here to work. I don't let you bother cook while she is making our dinner, do I?" Lady Stanford gently reminded her son of the difference in class between himself and the servants, and Eliza felt a slight kernel of regret that things could not be as Edward imagined them. Still, it was a trifling sadness, one that paled against the greater joy of being accepted as a servant of the manor. Eliza didn't even need to ask to know that the job would pay better than her leech collecting. Even if it didn't, just the simple pleasure of working indoors, in the warm and not being eaten alive by bloodsucking worms, was enough to recommend her to the job.

"You can trust me, Edward... your mother's offer is very gracious and more than I could have ever hoped for. I should be very happy about working in the kitchens." Eliza smiled to both mother and son, nervousness setting in after having again spoken to Edward in so informal a manner.

"Then it's settled," Lady Stanford said, clapping her hands together. "Edward, you need your rest so lie down and get some sleep. Miss Thorn, let us take you down to the kitchens and see if we might find you a uniform and I shall write to your parents, explaining things."

"Thank you very much, M'lady," Eliza said, quickly moving after the woman, a grin plastered on her face as she considered how well she might look in a proper maid's dress.

"You will come back later on to visit me, won't you?" Edward asked.

"Get some rest now," Lady Stanford answered on Eliza's behalf, closing the door firmly behind her. Though far more civil and pleasing than her husband and eldest son, Eliza could tell that propriety and proper boundaries of class still mattered very highly to Lady Stanford, and she was surely eager to put a wedge between her and the friendship Edward seemed to be forming with her. Eliza felt it something of a pity; she did quite like Edward. However, she knew in her heart that it was not right and proper for them to be friends, as he wished, and that the opportunity presented to her to work in the manor was far and beyond what she could have expected for helping save the young man's life.

CHAPTER 5

Christmas - 1847

Edward never seemed to fully understand why a job in the kitchens of his home was so attractive to Eliza, but then he never needed to. When it came down to it, the youngest of the Stanford brothers was simply glad that Eliza was nearby and accessible to him whenever he wished to see her, which was far more often than was really good for him.

In the month leading up to Christmas, just as Eliza was being instructed on her role within the house, Edward became an almost permanent fixture of the servants' rooms and back passages of the manor, tailing Eliza like a puppy until he could be persuaded away. Lady Stanford became particularly adept at anticipating her son's visits to the kitchens and would often intercept him or else come down on a mythical 'errand' five minutes into his loitering by the sinks.

Eliza tried her best to deter Edward from coming down to see her too often, but it was hard going. The difficulty came from Eliza's own desire to spend time in Edward's company, to listen to his stories and hopes and dreams for the future. During their fearful and desperate retreat across the marshes, Eliza learned enough of the boy to know he was a good and pleasant kind of youth, but it was so much better talking to him without the fear of death hanging over them.

As she washed, stacked, dried, and put away dishes, cutlery and pans, Eliza heard all kinds of incredible things from Edward, becoming thoroughly absorbed with his world.

Edward's principal goal in life, and one that Eliza thoroughly approved of, was to become something apart from Martin. He did not like to think of himself as needing to forever answer to his older brother, nor to be forced into a low profession like the military or the church as was expected of second sons. Edward spoke of one day owning a business, becoming a leader of industry with a fortune of his own that would see him free of his brother and never needing to ask for Martin's aid, or being forced to grovel for favours when his elder sibling became Earl.

Knowing that the other servants, the cook particularly, were always listening in whenever Edward came to speak to her, Eliza was always careful with her words and responses, but she felt confident enough to encourage Edward on his course, reasoning that none of the staff could berate her for encouraging the master to better himself. And, whenever Eliza feared Edward was lingering too long in her company and word of his visits might reach the ear of his father, Eliza would use the boy's own ambition to her advantage. She would subtly remind Edward that if he wished to become some paragon of industry and business, he would need to pay greater attention to education and learning. This would invariably be enough to send the impressionable and excitable boy on his way, rushing to his room or to find his tutor who kept a room on the estate while the family was visiting.

Eliza was glad she could be so positive an influence for Edward. Even the cook noted it. "That boy is full of grand plans and ambitions but none of the wherewithal to make them into a reality. But since you've come here, I've never seen the young master so attentive to his learning."

Even Lady Stanford, who remained always a little cautious of Edward's association with Eliza, owned that she was proving a positive influence and gifted her a shilling for the trouble. Eliza was pleased she could encourage Edward to better himself in such a way, but there was one thing she congratulated herself for above all else, something more important than Edward's education and focus on his studies. Any time Edward came down into the kitchens looking for Eliza it was another occasion where he was not being lured into absurd traps and tricks by his callous and malicious elder brother. Though rarely sent upstairs into the main rooms of the house, Eliza had nevertheless learned of all the ways Martin liked to get his younger brother in trouble, taking a kind of perverse glee in tormenting his sibling and abusing his too trusting and impetuous nature.

In the month leading up to Christmas, Edward had not once been sent to his father's office for falling for one of his brother's hijinks, nor been brought to harm by accepting some whimsical dare. Eliza liked to think she was shielding Edward from Martin's dark influence and machinations and she hoped she might continue to do so for a long time to come.

~

Christmas Day was strange for Eliza that year. She woke early, before the hour of four. She was roused by the housekeeper, Mrs Lynch, and was downstairs helping to prepare breakfast, lunch, and dinner, all before the Stanfords had risen from their beds.

To her surprise and joy, Eliza found that the servants had been gifted their own generous Christmas day's breakfast and lunch, enjoying sausage, egg and bacon for her breakfast and the promise of her own small bird roast late in the evening, once the day's tasks were done and the Stanford family went to bed.

Eating her breakfast with relish, Eliza could not help but think about what she was missing out on. As a servant on the Earl's estate, she now only saw her family once a month, when she was given a free day to go down into the village. It was made clear to her that she would be needed for work on Christmas Day and Eliza had first baulked at the idea of spending Christmas apart from her family. But the warm comfort of her servant's room in the manor, the hot cooked breakfast, the pay, it all reassured her that she was where she should be, and she consoled herself that she would see her parents again soon enough and that their own Christmas feast would be made a little more extravagant this year by the extra income she was bringing in. She knew her mother and father were extremely grateful for her and the new position she had landed for herself, and there was hope that, in a few years, her station within the Stanford Household would elevate higher and she might soon be earning even more than her own father.

Lost in her thoughts, Eliza jumped when she heard a harsh clap just behind her head. "Out of your daydreams now," Mrs Lynch said, her tone sharp but not horrible. "The master gave us a generous breakfast so we'd have the energy for the work ahead, not so we could loiter and grow fat on our stools."

"Yes, Ma'am," Eliza said. She looked about her, seeing that the rest of the staff had all just about finished their Christmas breakfast. Servants in immaculate uniforms were draining the last of their tea, handkerchiefs held under their chins lest they spill a brown stain on their shirts. Meanwhile, the kitchen staff were all moving to their posts, the cook beginning to bark her own orders of what food needed to be prepared first and when everything should be put in the oven.

Realising just how behind the others she was, Eliza stuffed the last of her sausage into her mouth along with a sliver of bacon and toast. Her cheeks were puffed out comically as she tried to chew and swallow it all down. She rushed about the table, gathering up the dirtied plates and cups, preparing for a day chained to the sink. On any given day, there was always a lot of washing up to be done, but for Christmas Day, Eliza knew the processions of pots, pans and plates would likely never cease. She set herself to her work, though, without fuss or complaint, idly imagining how Edward would be enjoying his day and wondering if he would appreciate all the work that she and the other servants were putting into making his and the rest of the Stanford family's Christmas Day truly exceptional. She knew her parents would be praying for her and the thought comforted her as she rolled up her sleeves.

∼

The day ran fast and slow together. Eliza certainly felt the strain of the day's chores as she was forced to confront an ever-growing pile of dishes and utensils. It seemed like any time she came close to clearing the sink a fresh batch of pans would be brought over and she would invariably receive some scolding from the cook for being too far behind. Eliza would heave a sigh, wipe the sweat off her brow with her forearm and then plunge her hands back into the dirty water as she returned to scrubbing and cleaning.

The day ran its course, Eliza learning to tell the time as much by the food being sent out from the kitchens as from the clock. The most intensive part of her day came in the evening, just as the Earl and his family were sitting down for their Christmas Dinner. Eliza was amazed at the sheer variety of dishes sent up. A myriad of appetisers and starters, a wide selection of meats for the main course, including salmon, duck, pheasant, venison, beef, and goose. Then, there was a multitude of deserts which she had been told were the highlight of the meal for the two boys. While the family upstairs ate, Eliza kept on scrubbing and cleaning, her work doubling as the plates and cutlery were brought down from each course.

As she worked, Eliza often looked back at the central table of the kitchen, noticing how much had been left by the family. The salmon had barely been touched and there was still a sizeable cut of beef left on the silver tray. The pheasant and the goose were picked clean but there was enough food left to feed at least three other families and Eliza was relieved when she learned that the leftovers would contribute to hers and the other servants' Christmas dinner shortly thereafter.

∽

At around ten o'clock, the servants began to gather to enjoy their own well-earned Christmas meal. Eliza, at only twelve years of age, was five years younger than any of the other servants in the household. Because of this and because she was a relative newcomer to the house, she did not have many friends amongst the staff, but she still enjoyed the spirited camaraderie and goodwill as she sat around the table with the other servants. All congratulated themselves at having made it through another Christmas Day, the cook apologised for ruling over the staff like a tyrant, and all relaxed and toasted their accomplishments before returning to their remaining duties or to bed.

Eliza, after washing up the last plates and bowls used by the staff for their supper, went to bed happy and proud. It had been an odd sort of Christmas for her, but it was good all the same. If she had one complaint about the whole day, it was that Edward had not come down to visit her even once during the whole day.

She imagined Edward would have been told by his mother not to get in the way or perhaps his excitable attitude had seen him too distracted by new presents to remember to go and see her. There were countless reasons why he might have shunned her, and Eliza only hoped it was by accident, not design.

Opening the door to her room, the young girl closed her eyes and stretched. Letting out a yawn, she staggered in the vague direction of her bed, not even caring to take off her clothes immediately. Without even opening her eyes, she let her body fall face-first onto the mattress, letting out a contented sigh as she spread her arms wide and embraced the warm, plush sheets.

"Sounds like you've had a long day."

Eliza's eyes opened at once and she gave a shriek as the unexpected voice intruded upon her moment of serene calm. Though dressed, she reflexively pulled the sheet covers over herself, staring in astonishment at the figure waiting for her in the corner of the room. She relaxed when she saw it was only Edward, and her cheeks flushed from both the embarrassment at having screamed and the slight thrill at having the young master steal into her room so late in the night. Of course, thrilling and touching though his visit was, it also made her fearful.

"What are you doing here?" Eliza hissed, looking nervously to her bedroom door in case one of the other servants had heard her shriek and might come running.

"Why I came to give you your Christmas present, of course," Edward said with a grin. He bounced across the room, holding something behind his back as he made his way to her.

"A Christmas present? You didn't! I haven't got you anything."

"I wouldn't have expected you to. You spend every moment of the day chained to the kitchen sink, the only present you could have ever got me would be a clean spoon," Edward joked cheerfully as he sat on the bed next to Eliza, clearly holding something tightly in his right hand. Whatever he had got her, it was very small indeed.

"Well, you still shouldn't have gone to the trouble for me, and you certainly shouldn't have stolen into my room in the dead of night like this," Eliza hissed. She wanted to relax, wanted to enjoy Edward's company alone; they so rarely had the opportunity, but that came with risks.

"Oh, don't be such a worrywart," Edward chided. "Here, if you're so worried about things, I can just give you your present and be on my way. I know we'll have more time to talk tomorrow. Mama can't keep me out of the kitchens forever... she'll probably be spending much of tomorrow lounging in a chair complaining of stomach cramps."

"I can't say I'm surprised after the amount of food sent up to you today. There was enough to feed Denton town," Eliza owned with a smile.

"Well, Merry Christmas, Eliza, I hope you'll think of this present as my own personal thank you for saving me back in the marshes the other month. You really were my guardian angel that day."

Eliza blushed at the comment. She knew she should say something, try and swat away the boy's compliments and downplay the role she had played in his rescue. At the same time, she relished his words and wanted to accept them.

Unable to find the words for that moment, Eliza remained still and quiet as Edward brought his hand to hers and slipped something delicate and metal into her palm. Eliza looked down at their conjoined hands, feeling a slight fluster and quickening of her heartbeat as she looked at them joined together. It was such a simple act and yet, for her, it was more important and joyous than any present the young master might have fashioned for her.

Just as she thought Edward might pull away, Eliza was stunned to see him lean in closer. Her eyes widened in astonishment and her head moved suddenly. What was surely meant as an affectionate kiss on the cheek was suddenly undone. Edward's lips pressed to Eliza's, his own eyes widening as they found themselves suddenly engaged in so intimate an act. Edward immediately withdrew, jumping off the bed as though it had suddenly caught fire. His face was beet red, and his eyes could no longer look directly at Eliza as he blundered backward toward her door.

"W... well, as I said, I really hope you like the trifle I got for you. It was the best I could do at such short notice, but I think it will do. I didn't mean to disturb your night and I hope you had a good Christmas, despite washing up all day." Edward's mouth was running away with him, trying to give voice to every panicked thought that entered his mind as he fought to deflect attention from the kiss they had so unexpectedly shared together on the bed.

"Goodnight Edward. Thank you for the present and Merry Christmas." Eliza offered the young master a warm smile, surprised at how still and tranquil she remained. She was flustered to be sure. There was a pleasant feeling of butterflies in her stomach and a heightened awareness of everything around her. But, somehow, the kiss had sent her to a dreamy haze of serenity that kept her mind easy and controlled as Edward blustered and blundered his way to the door.

Eliza waited till Edward was out of the room and the door closed before daring to look down at the present he had so unexpectedly bought her. She relished the surprise, feeling the fragile weight of the thing in her hand for a time and trying to guess at what it could possibly be. When at last she turned her hand and opened her fingers, the silver fancy resting in her palm stole her breath away.

There, resting in her trembling hand, sat a beautiful and delicate silver necklace complete with a pendant, also of silver, shaped like an angel. Compared to the jewels that Lady Stanford wore, the necklace was nothing more than a bauble, a trinket, not even worth the lady's notice, but to Eliza it was everything. Just looking at the craftsmanship that went into the chain and into the sculpted wings of the angelic figure dangling from it, Eliza could scarce imagine the worth of the gift. Certainly, it was more expensive than anything her mother could afford, and she knew instinctively she should never show the gift to her mother or father. Though kind parents, they were also practical. If she were ever to show them the gift Edward had given her, their first thought would be to pawn it away and put the money to more useful ends.

Eliza sighed, her finger trailing the silvered outline of the angel, biting her bottom lip as she tried to suppress tears of sheer joy and happiness. She had never felt such contentment in her entire life, never felt so valued and cared for. And added to that feeling was that unintentional, but not at all regretted, kiss with Edward.

A second sigh. Eliza let herself fall back onto the bed, clutching the necklace close to her heart and closing her eyes tight. In her mind, she found herself revisiting that accidental kiss, smiling as she remembered Edward's flushed cheeks and awkward ramblings that followed after. It was so very like him and quite adorable.

Only once did thoughts of propriety intrude upon her musings. As Eliza heard the chimes from the hallway clock sound midnight, she remembered that she still had work to attend to on the morrow and could not afford to be made lazy or lethargic from a lack of sleep. Clutching the necklace in her hands as younger girls might clutch a cherished doll, Eliza closed her eyes, reminding herself that the kiss would likely not be repeated, that this stolen moment alone was a one-off magical event she would forever cherish but could never reasonably think to see re-enacted in the future.

CHAPTER 6

Christmas 1852

Five years of working in the Stanford house had seen Eliza blossom from a shy, uncertain girl of the marshes to a respected and valued maid. Her days scrubbing dishes in the kitchens were far behind her, and she found herself more and more entrusted with work in the main house. In the mornings, Eliza would go to Lady Stanford's room with a pot of tea, and afterward, make her bed and tidy the room when her ladyship was at breakfast. During the day, she was responsible for cleaning the family rooms as needed, working to a steady rota, ensuring surfaces were dusted, polished, and waxed as required. It was a pleasing task and easier than her former work in the kitchens. Better still, it paid more, and Eliza found herself an equal in fortunes to her own father.

Convinced that Eliza would have her pick of any man in the village when it came time to be wed, though she was just seventeen, her mother had begun putting money aside from her daughter's generous wage as a dowry for when she married. Eliza did not care for such talk, though. It unsettled her deeply, not least because her mother always seemed to speak of marriage as if it was just around the corner. On the days when Eliza was free to come down from the manor and spend time with her family, her mother would always quiz her on what boys in the village she liked and extolling the virtues of those she thought would make suitable matches for her. It did not occur to the woman that Eliza spent almost all her time up at the manor and thus barely knew any of the lads in the village her mother spoke of. Eliza lived in an altogether different world now—a kind of limbo between the life she had known as a common leech picker and the life of luxury and circumstance that could be found at the Earl's home.

There was another reason why Eliza did not care to think of marriage or be drawn into her mother's musings about the future. Of course, though she was still years from having to consider a husband for herself, Eliza knew that there was yet another reason why she did not care for her mother's fanciful ideas for her future.

Edward.

Eliza did not get to see her friend often, but the moments they shared together and the memory of that one accidental kiss shared on a Christmas night long ago had stayed with her down the years. She could not shake free of it, nor did she want to. She kept it as a treasured secret, deep down inside. Even Edward did not know how much that moment had meant to her. In the years since, he had never once made mention of that night or the kiss they had shared, and Eliza did not wish to ruin their friendship by drawing attention to it.

There were, Eliza knew, many reasons why she should forget that night, or at least the part of it she treasured above all else. Edward was the son of an earl. Even if only a second son, Eliza knew he would be expected to marry a girl of breeding and respectability, not a leech collector he had found on the fens. For most of the year, Edward was in London, only coming to the family's country estate for certain holidays and special occasions. Though he spoke often of his life in the city and had never once mentioned women, Eliza was sure there had to be many a girl of that fair city who could catch his eye. She pictured them with their hair done up in a regal fashion, all bouncing curls and luxurious locks. Their dresses would be arresting and accentuate beautiful, unblemished skin. Their hands and fingers would be soft too, not cracked and calloused from work and labour as hers were. Eliza pictured such women from time to time with a mix of jealousy and resignation, wondering just when her friend and confidant would come home with tales of having fallen in love with a beautiful heiress. It had not happened yet, but Edward was growing older, just as she was, and Eliza doubted he would remain ignorant of the fairer sex for much longer.

∼

It was Christmas Eve, and the house held in a state of excited readiness for the festivities to come. The servants stayed up late ensuring all the preparations were ready for the morrow. Eliza and her fellow servant, Isabelle, left to make ready the dining room and breakfast room for the next day. The girls were about halfway through their appointed task when there was a knock heard at the door. Normally, so polite a gesture would signify the arrival of another servant, so both Isabelle and Eliza were greatly shocked when they found none other than Edward himself standing in the doorway, rapping lightly on the door to get their attention. Both women immediately ceased their polishing and dusting and received the master with polite curtseys.

"I hope I am not intruding," Edward said, his voice a little nervous.

"This is your home, Edward, and we are your servants," Eliza reminded him, offering the young man a warm smile. "You know you don't have to knock or apologise if you need anything." It was a gentle admonishment and Eliza truly had no real desire to see Edward change. Something was pleasing about the way he comported himself about her and the respect he showed others beneath his station, that she could not help but admire.

"Well, I do know Christmas Eve is a busy time for you all and I should not wish to interrupt you if you have much left to arrange but... well, I wondered if I could take a moment of your time, Miss Thorn."

Eliza looked to Isabelle, feeling a slight discomfort as the other servant tried in vain to hold back an amused smirk. Eliza had eyes and ears. She knew that as the years had passed some of the servants had paid more attention to her friendship with the young man and a few had begun to tease her in earnest on their so-called 'first-flush romance.' Eliza tried to ignore the gossipers, but it wasn't easy. Taking in Isabelle's excited and amused look at that moment, Eliza was certain she would be made to suffer more than a few rumours if she stepped out the room with Edward now. For all this, it was a price she was willing to pay.

"If you require me, I shall, of course, attend at once," Eliza said in the proper fashion, putting down the silvered candlestick she was holding, returning it to the table. She gave a nod to Isabelle, trying to shut out the other maid's broadening grin from her mind as she followed Edward out into the hall.

"You know, pulling me away from my work like this is going to cause me trouble one of these days," Eliza warned as soon as the door was closed and she found herself able to talk with her friend in the easy, casual manner they had always preferred.

"I know. Ordinarily I would not look to tear you from your duty or risk the servants telling mother I had pulled you from your chores, but I just had to tell you something."

Eliza drew in a sharp breath. For some reason, Edward's suggestion of an urgent revelation conjured in her mind again the image of some other woman in London, young and beautiful, met at a party or gala in the summer and whom Edward had quickly fallen for. She tried to keep her calm, adopting a tense smile as she nodded attentively. Eliza waited for a moment, eyes narrowing a little when Edward did not immediately come forward with his secret. Their walk down the corridor stopped, Eliza turning to look to her friend directly. As she studied Edward's face, she realised her initial fear and impression had been wrong. His face was ashen, his lips drawn thin, and shoulders hunched. He looked melancholy, as if someone had died.

"Goodness Edward, what is it?" Eliza said, her voice trembling a little to see him so out of sorts. "What can see you so glum on Christmas Eve?"

"It is something that will come with the new year, something I thought to keep to myself to spare you. But… well, I don't think I can keep it a secret anymore, not from you."

Eliza bit her bottom lip, feeling tears well in her eyes even though she did not yet know why.

"It seems my brother has been conniving to get rid of me again."

"Have you been fighting again?" Eliza asked, her voice fractured with worry. In the past years, the boyish rivalry between Martin and Edward had grown steadily. No longer confined to pranks and dares, Martin had grown notably jealous of all Edward had accomplished. Putting his mind to his studies through Eliza's encouragement, Edward had come to exceed Martin in his schooling despite the age difference. This had been a source of frustration for Martin, and Eliza understood the elder's temper had increased in correlation to Edward's accomplishments.

"We have not been fighting," Edward assured with a sigh. "But Martin has been talking with father, bending his ear about the need for me to make a career for myself."

"Well, what business is it of his? Your father should know that with your academics and accomplishments you are perfectly capable of getting any kind of job you should wish."

"True, but Martin suggested to father it would be in my best interests for him to buy me a commission."

"A commission? You mean... you are for the army?"

Edward shook his head and shrugged in resignation. "It was a brilliant move by Martin, I will give him that much. He knows our father is interested in lineage and pride. An Earl's son serving with distinction in Her Majesty's army —what could be more glorious?"

"But... you must have some kind of choice in the matter, you could refuse?" Eliza swallowed, fighting grim mental pictures of Edward out on a frontier of the empire, bloodied and dying. "You must convince him that you do not want this."

"I spoke with my father, but it did little good. My commission was bought and paid for at great cost to him and I cannot now refuse my posting without doing significant damage to our family name."

"So, hang your family name!" Eliza said, pushing forward and grabbing Edward by the lapels, all propriety and manners lost. She needed to hold him then, to feel she had him anchored to her. If it would stop him from leaving, she would gladly keep him held for days, months.

"Well, isn't this a naughty picture..." A voice from the farther end of the hall caused both Eliza and Edward to turn. Eliza felt her whole body stiffen and her lip curl in anger as she found their conversation intruded upon by the very man who was responsible for his brother's unwanted commission.

"Edward, I know it is tempting to go sneaking around with the servants for a bit of sport, but you really shouldn't carry on like this out in the halls where anyone could see… Imagine the gossip." Martin wore a malicious smile as he folded his arms and waited for his younger brother to step back from Eliza.

Edward complied with his brother's request, drawing back a step and looking to Martin with a steely resolve. "I do not believe you can do me any harm here, brother. You know I have never made my friendship with Miss Thorn a secret. Father may not be all together approving of the association, but it is known to him. And I do not 'make sport' with servants like they are extensions of our property." Edward held himself tall against his brother, not flinching as Martin stalked forward.

"You should get your sport in while you may, little brother," Martin goaded. "Once in the army, you won't have much chance to enjoy yourself otherwise."

Eliza pursed her lips, fighting the urge to make some rebuke at Martin. It would be her job if she said anything out of turn and speaking out might hurt Edward even more.

Edward kept his cool remarkably, not rising to his brother no matter how his sibling tried to provoke him. "Are you done posturing now, brother?" Edward asked. "I have more I wish to say to Miss Thorn and do not much care if you go running to father. So why don't you run along and leave me to my business."

Martin scowled, grabbing Edward by the collar and leaning in close. Eliza gasped, fearing he might strike his brother. His hands were balled into fists, but he did not lash out. "You should look to be more obedient, little brother," Martin growled. "When I become Lord of this manor, I will not forget these insults, your rudeness. You had better learn to change your tune soon or I may be forced to see you cut off when I take charge of the estate."

Edward smirked a little, his amused smile causing Martin's brow to knot in confusion. Realising, perhaps, that he could not intimidate his brother, Martin gave the pair one last withering look then stalked away down the passage. Edward did not even bother to watch him go, just turned about and continued on his own way, putting an arm about Eliza in a gesture of solidarity.

"He gets worse every year, I swear," Edward mumbled to himself.

"He's intimidated by you," Eliza said, her own voice clipped, frustrated. "He knows you can be more than he ever will and seeks to do all he can to keep you down."

"And to think outshining my brother was always my dream." Edward sighed. "Now look where it's got me—a surprise commission with the military that I can't back away from. I can't decide if Martin just wants me sent overseas where he doesn't have to see my face or if he genuinely hopes I get myself killed out there."

Eliza did not answer. She did not want to believe that any brother could be so completely self-centred and vile as to want their own brother dead, but then Martin always seemed to surprise her.

"So, there is no way you can turn down this commission at all then?" Eliza asked again, keeping her mind centred on what was most important at that moment.

"No way that I can see," Edward said. "There is the dishonourable option, bring shame to my family name and my own. I am sure Martin would be equally happy with that outcome. Perhaps father might cut me off."

"You would survive it. You have talent and worth enough that any employer in London would wish to take you on. You can stand on your own two feet and show Martin that you do not need him or your family's name and fortunes to back you up."

"If it were just Martin, I might be very tempted to do such a thing," Edward confessed with a nod. "As it is, I do not want to disappoint Father or Mother in such a way. The rest of the world may have evolved, but for landed families such as ours, there are still set ways and traditions. It is, sadly, still the custom for the second son of a noble house to serve for queen and country and to go against my father's wishes and refuse to accept a commission could be damaging to both my name and our family's... At least within the circles we frequent."

Eliza nodded. She did not much care for Lord Stanford. He was not cruel, like Martin, but he was distant and cold, seeing his children as investments who should follow set paths and lines he made for them. He was, however, Edward's father and she could understand her friend not wishing to disappoint him.

"Well, this is not the kind of news I should have liked to hear this Christmas," Eliza said, letting out a forlorn sigh. She could still feel tears threatening to spill from the corners of her eyes, but she held herself in check.

"I am sorry," Edward whispered, his head bowed in contrition. "I truly did think to bring you the news after Christmas, but it was just... you are my dearest and oldest friend, and I could not keep it from you."

"No, I understand, and I am glad you told me," Eliza said with a nod. "Hard though it is to hear, I would rather know of it now while you still have time here on the estate than on New Year's Day just before you are set to leave for who knows where... how long even will you be away?"

Edward shook his head again. "It is difficult to say. My father ambushed me with the commission just the other week, his idea of a surprise Christmas present. I have still to look over the finer details of the posting."

Eliza nodded, her feet failing her as she came to a forlorn stop once more. A sob escaped her lips and she put her hands to her face to hastily wipe the first tears that she could feel running down her cheek. "I am sorry... I know I should be stronger... But I just... I don't want you to leave. Your visits here... your being here..."

"Our time together is precious to me too," Edward replied, He turned to look directly at Eliza again, his hand reaching for her cheek as he wiped away the tears that ran there. "I shall be safe. Martin may be conspiring to send me far from England, but we are not at war, and an officer's life is not so perilous as he would like to think. And I do not wish our friendship to suffer because of my absence."

"You can be assured it will not," Eliza replied, summoning her courage. "I will be thinking of you always. I'll pray for your safety and I'll—"

"—I meant that I shall not let months go by without any correspondence between us," Edward corrected with a warm smile. "You can depend on me to write to you regularly and I hope that you will offer me the same courtesy."

"Are you sure that is appropriate?" Eliza asked, her eyes glancing past Edward again lest anyone else was about to listen in.

"I know my father and mother would not like to hear of it and so I have a plan to ensure I can write to you without anyone having to know or make an objection."

Eliza tried to smile. It was a wan, trembling smile but she was just about able to hold it. She would rather Edward not leave at all; would rather he stay and take whatever ramifications and censure he would receive for refusing his commission. But she understood why he had to go. Even if he did stand up to his father, ending up disowned, Eliza knew the outcome would ultimately be the same. He would be cast out of the manor, and she should likely not see him again. All options before them were bad and she could only hope that Edward was choosing the best course for himself.

CHAPTER 7

Christmas - 1854

To speak truthfully, I am grateful for the opportunity to be returning home and to be once more able to see your face in person. Is that wrong of me? I know my thoughts should be with my father and his condition, but am I not allowed also to relish the chance to see my closest friend once more? Your letters, alongside those of my mother, are the one constant I have out here, and I do not know what I would do without them. Still, I yearn for more.

I look forward to my return to Denton and pray that I might be with you again in time for Christmas. So long as the tides are favourable and we receive no new orders that might impede my return, all should be well.

Look forward to my return as I look forward to seeing you again.

Yours,

Peter Alton

Eliza drew in a deep breath as she read the last of the letter again. She held the missive in her right hand, her left gently caressing the necklace Edward had given her so many years ago now. The polished silver of the chain had dulled with age, but there was still some sparkle on the edge of the angel pendant. Where Eliza made a habit of rubbing the pendant's feet for encouragement, the thing had taken on a lustrous shine. It could hardly be a surprise since she toyed with the trinket almost every night, reading and rereading at leisure the deluge of letters she had received from Edward down the last few years, each one signed under the pseudonym, Peter Alton.

Peter Alton was a useful cover for Edward and Eliza. To the staff who delivered Eliza her letters or who caught her reading from time to time, Peter Alton was a friend from the village who had moved away and who took time to write to Eliza now they could no longer hope to see one another in person. If the steward and the other servants were to know that Eliza received monthly letters from Edward Stanford, they would surely go to the man's parents and alert them. Tolerant though Lady Stanford and Lord Stanford had been of their son's friendship with her, it would no doubt alarm them to know that he kept such regular correspondence with one of the servants. They were far better off believing that Eliza's friendship with Edward was a fair-weather kind, only blossoming for short periods when their son was home at the manor. Anything more could create a scandal. Eliza also often prayed that God would forgive them for their deceit. Though it seemed necessary her conscience still smarted in the knowledge that she was not being entirely truthful.

Another use for Edward's pseudonym was in keeping Eliza's mother from pushing any harder on the prospect of marriage. To Mrs Thorn, Peter Alton was known as a former servant of the manor, one whom Eliza had taken fondly to and kept up a correspondence with since he left to take on a career in the army. Through the ruse of Peter Alton, Eliza was able to stave off talk of marriage and courtship with the local men of Denton, dropping subtle hints to her mother that someday she might expect a proposal from Peter. It was a lie that was both convenient for Eliza but also somewhat painful to tell.

Growing up, Eliza had always heard the phrase, 'Absence makes the heart grow fonder,' but she hadn't appreciated the cruel truth of that proverb until Edward had taken up his commission and departed England for countries and adventures unknown.

It was a strange thing. In many respects, Eliza was closer to Edward now than she had ever been. His monthly letters meant that she heard from him far more often than when they were children. In those days, Eliza could go three or four months at a time waiting for the Stanford family to come up from London to enjoy their country home. Still, though she was certainly able to correspond with Edward more freely than she ever had in the past, his physical absence from her life was felt keenly, and some days she feared she might forget his face were he to return to the manor unannounced.

Still clutching the letter in one hand, Eliza pushed up from her bed and moved to the window. She took a moment to look out into the dark winter's night outside. A full moon cast its silver light upon fresh virgin snow, almost shin deep. Christmas Eve was upon them again, and Eliza had to accept that, despite Edward's optimistic hopes in his last letter, he was not now going to be able to fulfil his promise of returning home for the holiday season. It was a sadness, not only for Eliza but also for Edward himself. His father's health had declined steadily in the last years, and she knew that Lady Stanford had written to Edward several times, urging him to find a way to return home to visit lest the worst should come to pass.

A knock on her bedroom door startled Eliza, and she bit her bottom lip as she looked at the letter in her hand. Despite being signed in Edward's pseudonym, she still felt incredibly subconsciously guilty to be caught with the missive, and she rushed over to her dressing table, shoving the letter inside along with the others she had kept down the years. She ran her hands through her hair, trying to tame the loose dark strands into a more acceptable bun.

"Yes, come in," Eliza called, eyes still darting straight back to the drawer where she kept her letters. She calmed a bit when Isabelle entered, frowning to see her friend and fellow maid still about at so late an hour.

"Is there some trouble? Is there a candlestick somewhere we forgot to polish for tomorrow's dinner?" Eliza asked, shooting her friend a smile. Isabelle did not reciprocate.

"Don't joke around, Eliza. We're liable to be up half the night, I shouldn't wonder. I just know I'll be yawning all through Christmas Day."

"What on earth has happened?" Eliza asked, not liking her friend's ominous suggestion.

"Martin Stanford has happened," Isabelle replied, taking care the door was closed before looking to bad mouth her employer. "Martin and the so-called friends he invited to share Christmas with him had an impromptu party in the drawing-room… then in the billiards room, and then in the breakfast room…"

Eliza groaned as she imagined the scene. "Do I dare ask the state of the rooms?" Eliza asked, her body tensing as she braced herself for the bad news.

"The billiard table is ruined, whiskey and rum spilt all over it. The steward is looking to see if we can have the surface recovered and replaced before morning, but it will all depend on if we have any spare surface. The carpets in the drawing room and breakfast room saw the worst of it and we need to get down there at once to help clean them and prevent any stains from settling."

Eliza nodded, grabbing her apron as she followed Isabelle out the door and into the corridor. "What a way to see in Christmas Day."

"If any of the men left a half glass of whiskey lying around, we might have a cheeky libation to bolster ourselves as we work, Isabelle suggested.

"Tempting, but I would not wish to bring my lips near anything Martin Stanford has handled." Eliza and Isabelle both giggled as they went down the stairs to see to their work.

∾

Many were needed to help clear the mess Martin Stanford and his four friends had created downstairs. The maids and servants attending to the task were quickly dispatched to separate rooms, Eliza found herself somewhat dismayed at having to clean stains from the breakfast room rugs by herself. She would have much preferred the work if she had Isabelle or someone else to speak to, but fate denied her.

Edward was away, and Eliza was seeing in the first minutes of Christmas Day scrubbing stains from the carpets in the dark. It was enough to make her question why she even stayed on at the Stanford house anymore. True, the pay was good. Still, the only reason she truly wished to remain at the manor was for those days when she could see Edward and there had been no such meeting in almost four years now. As she scowled at the stains on the rug, she wondered if she should look for opportunities in another stately home.

Lost in her thoughts and rumination, Eliza was startled when the breakfast room door opened. She looked up, expecting to see one of the servants, but was disappointed. Stumbling into the room was none other than Martin Stanford. His eyes were bloodshot and unfocused, and he wobbled on his feet, quickly staggering into the doorframe. He looked to Eliza, squinting hard as though struggling to make out just who was bent down on the floor, cleaning.

"Oh... looks like I've found Edward's favourite toy."

Eliza stood, eyes trained down at her feet and wearing a grim expression as she waited on her master's pleasure.

"You have any plans for Christmas this year? Another year without Edward, I reckon you must be getting pretty lonely."

"I am quite all right, thank you," Eliza said, her voice clipped and curt.

"You *are* quite all right," Martin said, leering a little as he staggered into the room toward her.

Though she knew her place and what was expected of her, Eliza could not help but flinch, drawing back a step as Martin moved toward her with a glint in his eyes that truly frightened her.

"You know, with Edward away, seems you could use a new friend," Martin cooed, inching ever closer.

Eliza could not run. She held her ground, trying not to breathe in the reeking stench of Martin's alcohol-laden breath as he leaned into her.

"I am quite all right for company, sir. I have my duties to keep me busy and I would not wish to deprive you of your rest."

"Then why not come upstairs and rest with me?" Martin whispered, putting a hand around Eliza's waist while the other played with her hair. Her body had turned as stiff as a board, unable to run, unsure how to fight, unwilling to give in. A silent prayer passed her lips for God's protection.

"This is a pretty thing," Martin mumbled, eyes glancing down at the pendant that shimmered softly in the low light. Eliza sucked in a breath, chiding herself for forgetting to stow the necklace under her uniform when Isabelle had come up to fetch her. Once again, she made no answer to Martin, just remained still and silent, praying the man would grow bored of her and wander away in search of more alcohol to help spirit him into unconsciousness.

"A pretty silver bauble like this, I bet you did not receive this from anyone in your family. Might this be a gift from Edward?"

Eliza remained silent, her breathing shallow and frightened.

"You know, I could cover you with jewels, lavish you with riches beyond anything my brother could hope to gift you on his officer's salary."

"Why would you?" Eliza asked, finding her voice as she looked to Martin in confusion. "You don't even like me. You've despised my friendship with Edward from the first, insulted me the first night I met you."

"Back when you were a muddied leech digger come in out of the fens," Martin reminded. "I've eyes and I've watched you grow. You've blossomed into quite the appetising dish."

"I thank you, but I am not some Christmas entre," Eliza said, at last summoning up the will to push away from Martin just as his hands were beginning to wander down the small of her back.

Martin's leer twisted into that too familiar scowl of anger he always wore when denied something he felt was his. His eyes were alive with menace and Eliza feared for her safety as he straightened up and moved toward her. "You won't accept me because you're loyal to Edward… is that it? Did you exchange your true love vows before he went away to war and left you?"

"He never left me, and we never exchanged vows," Eliza returned, struggling to maintain any composure now against the odious man who would one day become master of the house.

A cough from the doorway caught Eliza's attention and she turned quickly, relief washing over her as she saw the steward standing there. While only another servant of the house, he reported to the Earl and Eliza knew that Martin could not lay a hand on her with him looking on.

"Apologies for the intrusion, My Lord. Is anything the matter?"

"Just come to get my drink," Martin replied, his scowl still very much in evidence even if his manner had improved. He stalked around Eliza, moving to the mantelpiece where one glass of brandy was left half drunk. He took the thing, knocking it back before shooting Eliza one last glance. "Good luck trying to clean up in here. Just remember, you can enjoy a much more rewarding evening if you would just lose that prudish attitude of yours."

Eliza pouted, noting the Steward's own awkward expression as the master showed himself out. To her relief the steward lingered in the doorway for a time, making sure that Martin did not double back. It gave her the confidence to continue her work. Wanting to put the dreadful encounter from her mind, Eliza moved back to the carpet stain and began to scrub at it all the harder, working out her frustrations as she did so.

There was no staying in Stanford Manor now, she told herself. The Earl was not long for the world, and she dreaded what might become of her when Martin took control. His lecherous nature and wandering eye were well known among the female staff, but this was the first time Eliza had been subject to his wolfish gaze. She did not wish to experience it again.

Working into the early hours to repair the damage from the party, Eliza set her mind to the year ahead. As soon as Christmas was done, she would apply for new employment in another stately home. She did not mind moving away, and she could still correspond with Edward through letters so long as she told him where such correspondence should be sent. Her path set, Eliza tidied the last of the things in the breakfast room, determined that she would not find herself doing the same one year hence.

CHAPTER 8

Christmas 1855

For a year, Eliza had heard nothing from Edward. His letter promising to be home in time for the previous Christmas was the last she had received from him and, as she understood it, the last anyone had heard of him. Eliza's plans to leave Stanford Manor were scuppered after that. Though desiring to move on from the manor and find employment away from Martin Stanford, she found herself lingering on. She came up with a dozen or more reasons for putting off her promised relocation. There was too much work to be done to apply for jobs elsewhere. The manor was not so bad a place to work most of the year when Martin was living the high life in London. Her parents would not wish to see her move to some far corner of the country where they could never hope to see her again. However, for all the reasons Eliza gave herself to explain why she had lingered for a whole extra year at Stanford Manor, there was only one reason that truly mattered to her. She needed to know what had become of Edward. If Eliza did not stay on in the Earl's employment, she knew she would be unlikely to hear any news of Edward, and she could not bear the thought of moving on with her life without knowing why he had so suddenly and inexplicably broken contact with her.

Eliza had many and varied ideas as to what had happened to her dear friend, none of which were particularly comforting to think upon. The first was the possibility that Edward had died in battle somewhere or maybe been captured by a hostile enemy of the British Empire. This, however, could be easily dismissed as Eliza knew the Earl and Lady Stanford would have been informed by the Military if their son was lost in battle.

With that notion quashed, new fears emerged.

Eliza began to fill her head with thoughts of Edward married. He had been away from England long enough. It was possible he had fallen in love with an exotic woman of the continent and lost all interest in her... not that he had that sort of interest in her to begin with. Whenever Eliza found her head filling with jealous imaginings of Edward with another woman, Eliza had to remind herself that he was not hers, nor could she ever reasonably expect him to be so. She was a servant, pulled out of the fens, just as Martin had pointed out the previous Christmas. Though forever grateful to her, there was no reason to suppose Edward might have fallen for her as she seemed to have done for him. It was an absurdity.

Even if Edward was not in love with another woman, Eliza began to wonder if her childhood friend had simply grown bored of her. Years apart might have made his feelings for her, even those of friendship, more distant and dispassionate. Perhaps, after failing to come home for four Christmases in a row, he had decided to abandon hopes of keeping ties with the past and looked to advance his future in the military.

There were so many plausible explanations as to why Edward had cut off all contact with Eliza and his parents and none of them were reassuring.

Still, Eliza remained at Stanford Manor. Unable to depart until she knew what had become of Edward, she began to view her employment in a grim fatalistic light. In the last year, Lord Stanford had grown weaker and evermore frail. Martin had been asked to step forward and take on virtually all the duties he could expect to be his when his father died, and he did not take to them well at all. His idea of being Earl amounted to little more than wearing his rank as a badge of office and spending the family's fortune however he pleased. Though Martin spent much of his time in London over the year, word of his exploits and errors filtered back to the manor.

Martin had spent a great deal of money looking to impress his friends. Rather than attending to the duties of stewardship of the estate that would be his, he chose to plunder it, digging deep into the family coffers and then selling off some of the Stanford family assets when he discovered their bank account was not infinitely deep.

Other servants started to pack their bags. None had left yet, but there was an understanding that certain members of the household would be let go soon as Martin sought to offset his lascivious expenses and decadent lifestyle. Certain portraits had already disappeared from the walls, sent down to London for auction from time to time.

In the manor, the servants asked themselves just when, if ever, Lord Stanford would intervene. Sick though he was, the staff had to assume he would not let his wayward heir trample over the family name so utterly while he was still alive. It had to be apparent, even to the dying old man that his eldest boy was not fit to look after the estate when he was gone. However, if the Earl was looking to do anything to correct Martin, he had made no obvious move toward such a goal yet.

To Eliza, it felt as if a dark and ominous cloud had gathered over the household and all within it. Either the darkness had to break and reveal clearer skies soon or, as seemed more and more likely, the rains would fall and wash away everything the Stanford family had ever built for themselves. And for all that, all she could care about was Edward, the need to know that he was well and safe, to understand why he had not written to her in so long.

Christmas came around again, though there was little cheer or evidence of it in the manor. With Lord Stanford now too sick to be moved up from London, the staff at the manor had been told that the family would not be travelling up to the country this year and that no feast or functions were to be expected. A few key members of the manor staff were summoned down to London to help oversee a smaller Christmas gathering, but Eliza was not among their number.

Left at the house with a skeleton staff, Eliza found herself on this Christmas eve ensuring the house was clean and tidy and that proper covers were put down on all the furnishings while the Manor endured its long quiet without a family to lighten its halls. The work was not particularly hard, but Eliza took her time through it. She lingered in each room, like some spectre or ghost who was wandering about and remembering a past life that was no longer hers. It was a melancholy feeling and Eliza found herself sighing over and over as she went on her way. In a very real and tangible sense, it felt to Eliza as though she were bidding goodbye to her life there. She had not had the heart to leave Stanford Manor on her own terms, but soon enough she would be forced to as Martin drove the family deeper and deeper downward.

"Are you about done?" a call came from the entryway. Eliza blinked several times, brought back to the present moment once again. She gave one last look to the room around her, finding it so strange to see the place so empty.

She then made her way to the door, patting the mantelpiece just once on her way as though it were some loyal dog.

Out in the hall, Isabelle and three other members of the household staff stood together, waiting for the chance to return down to the village to enjoy Christmas with their families. Eliza was aware she was holding them up, and she gave an apologetic smile to the group as she descended the staircase. She was only about halfway down the stairs when a knock at the front door caused them all to turn in surprise.

No one moved to answer immediately. On Christmas Eve, with the family away in London, there was no reason to be expecting visitors. A few of the servants groaned in exasperation, not wanting their leaving to be delayed further. One man moved slowly to the door, fishing in his pocket for the keys to open up. The banging at the main entrance continued, growing ever more impatient and incessant, and Eliza frowned. She could not for the life of her guess who had such urgent business at the manor on Christmas Eve unless…

Eliza bit her bottom lip, scarcely daring to hope that perhaps the late Christmas visitor could be Edward. Not having written to the family for so long it was possible he had no idea his family were wintering in London. He could have come directly to the manor, expecting his father and mother to be enjoying their traditional Christmas in the country.

Time seemed to slow as Eliza watched the front door, her mind filling with a hundred questions of how she should receive Edward if it really was him. Should she be grateful and pleased to see him alive and well, or should she be angered and demand to know how he could have so callously left her in the dark this past year?

The door opened and a figure stepped in from the cold. Just beyond the door, Eliza could see a stallion trotting about on the front lawn. Whoever the visitor was, he had travelled all the way through the winter cold on horseback. Their journey must have been awful, considering the snow, and Eliza could see the man struggling to pull off his thick gloves and the scarf that was wrapped around his face leaving only his eyes on show. Those eyes looked her way immediately and Eliza felt quite sure the stranger was there for her from that intense gaze.

"Miss Thorn, I am glad I have caught you. I wonder if we might talk, you and I?"

Eliza recognised the voice and her brow knotted in confusion as the man unwound the scarf from his face revealing his identity at last to her.

"Martin? I mean... Lord Stanford? What on earth are you doing here?"

"We did not expect to see you here this winter, Master," another of the servants piped up, the others quickly moving to attend the Lord, now they recognised him.

"I am afraid the house is all closed up, but we can have your room prepared and make you something warm to drink," another of the servants offered as everyone quickly snapped to attention.

"Please, just set a fire going in the drawing room if you please and give me a minute alone with Miss Thorn. I have something of the utmost importance I wish to speak with her on."

Eliza did not know what to make of Martin's sudden appearance and declaration. She could think of nothing in the world he would have to say to her that would warrant his travelling so far in the dead of winter. At a guess, she could only assume the master had word of Edward, but it would not be at all like him to go to the trouble of informing her of his brother.

"I shall help get the fire going in the drawing room and we can talk at once," Eliza said, finally. Though apprehensive and more than a little cautious, she could hardly deny the Lord. At least, by the look of him, he was not drunk on this occasion.

∽

A fire was made up in the drawing room and the white sheets quickly thrown off the chairs and tables. Many of the ornaments that normally decorated the room were missing, put away in boxes for safekeeping until the family returned, and this made the room feel most bare, almost skeletal to Eliza as she stood near the fire, watching Martin pace the room.

He was agitated, that much was certain. He crossed the floor in great strides, hands clasped tightly behind his back and looking to his pocket watch every few minutes as though he had another pressing engagement he really had to get to and was running late for.

Once the fire was lit and the room made ready, Martin shooed away the servants, refusing all offers of tea or sustenance. Eliza did not know what to make of it all and held herself in a defensive posture, her arms folded and her eyes watching Martin as a cornered rabbit watches the predatory fox.

"Perhaps you had better explain why you are here now?" Eliza suggested as the other servants at last left the room. Still remembering Martin's drunken advances from the previous year, Eliza felt her body grow tense at being left alone with the master. She prayed the other servants had the presence of mind to linger just outside the door, to not leave her completely alone with the man.

"I have come here with some news and... and also a proposition for you, Miss Thorn," Martin said, turning to look at her with a grave and serious expression. "First, I suppose it is only right I share with you the news." Martin drew in a deep breath, letting out an exaggerated sigh. His eyes drew down toward the floor and he solemnly bowed his head as his hands clasped together.

"I know how important my brother was to you, it is part of the reason I resolved to ride here tonight to inform you..."

"Inform me of what?" Eliza asked guardedly, shuddering at the grim portent of Martin's words and his manner at that moment.

"We have, I know, all been wondering why my brother cut off all contact with the family this last year and we now have the truth of things. He was struck down with a fever whilst abroad for much of the last year."

"No," Eliza replied, placing her hands to her mouth in shock.

"I am afraid so," Martin confirmed, moving forward with slow almost cautious steps, he seemed to be studying her expression, looking for signs of her feelings. Eliza wanted to cry, at the same time, she couldn't with Martin watching her so intently.

"How... How did it happen? Why didn't we learn of it sooner?"

"It was some form of influenza that kept him to his bed for the longest time. Much of the last year Edward spent wasting away in a hospital room. The doctors might have written to us and informed us of his condition, but he did not want to worry the family. It was so like him."

Eliza nodded a little. She could both accept Martin's words and couldn't at the same time. On the one hand, it did feel very much like Edward to not want to worry her or his parents. At the same time, he was wise enough to know that his long period of quiet would have caused panic and worry in and of itself. He also was not the kind to keep secrets. Eliza well remembered his inability to keep the news of his enlistment into the army to himself. If he truly were sick, she felt sure he would have confided in her.

"I know this must come as a shock to you, and my mother and father are taking the news none too well," Martin continued. His voice was calm, respectful, everything Eliza knew the man not to be. He reached out to her and put a consoling hand on her shoulder, the action causing Eliza to flinch and draw back.

"Please, do not touch me, sir," she begged, turning away from him and looking to the window. The light of the fire on the glass reflected her own face and Martin's shadow back at her and she watched his reflection carefully, eager for him not to draw any closer to her.

"I know I am probably the last person you would wish to hear this news from," Martin conceded, lowering his head in contrite apology. "We have not had the best of relationships in the past. In my youth I was obnoxious and rude to you and, last year, I know I acted out of turn."

Eliza said nothing, pursing her lips tightly as she tried to figure Martin out. Where could this apology and new-found goodness be coming from? Though it would have been nice to believe the man had finally found some moral compass and kernel of goodness, she hated to think it had taken his brother's death to sow a conscience in him.

"I have... acted irresponsibly in the past and I know I must do better by my family and by those I have wronged," Martin said. Even as he spoke there was something strange in his tone. The words came almost reluctantly, as though they left a sour taste in his mouth on coming out.

"If you are here to make an apology to me, you needn't bother," Eliza said. "Please do not take this the wrong way. I am grateful that you have taken the trouble to bring... bring me this news of Edward, but I am not able to forget the way you have behaved—both toward me and Edward. I certainly cannot think of such things now when I am trying to understand how Edward... how he could have..." Eliza felt her emotions threatening to spill over and she rallied herself as best she could. She wanted to scream, wanted to crumple up on the floor in a ball and hold tight the necklace she still wore religiously. But she would not break down in front of Martin, she would not give him the satisfaction of seeing her break apart and she would not let down her guard around him.

"I... I understand how you must feel," Martin continued, pushing closer to Eliza once more. She stiffened as she watched his reflection in the window, preparing to move if he came too close. "Believe me, I can understand the tumult of emotion that must be rushing through you to hear all of this so suddenly. But I feel I must tell you Edward's dying wish and... confess something I have long hidden from you."

Eliza turned around, her brow raised, and her lips pulled into a disbelieving grimace as she took in the man's words. She could not put her finger on the why of it, but everything Martin was saying felt so wrong to her. "What wish?" she asked incredulously.

Martin looked to Eliza, his face turning serious as he suddenly bent down before her on one knee. Eliza just stared at him in horror and utter confusion, the sight of him there before her so absurd that she could find no words.

"My brother cared for you so deeply, Miss Thorn. It was his fondest wish that you be looked after and cared for. He... he always felt he owed you a debt after you saved him from the fens."

"Please, please just stand up, sir," Eliza said, feeling her agitation rising as she struggled to accept Martin's present posture.

"Just hear me out, Eliza," Martin said, his voice momentarily carrying that barbed anger she was used to. His eyes glanced momentarily to the wall clock. "I... I know I was mean to you in my childhood, but that was because I did not wish to admit to my fascination and attraction to you. Last Christmas, drunk and reprehensible though my actions were, I realised for the first time how I truly feel for you, accepted the part of me that wished to make you my bride."

"Your bride?" Eliza repeated the words in astonishment and disdain. She tried to draw back again but this time Martin snagged her hands and forced her to remain before him.

"Please, Miss Thorn, won't you do me the honour of becoming my wife? It is so perfect. I can fulfil my brother's wish by looking after you, and I know you can help reform me and make me a better person, just as you once did with Edward. We both know I have failed to live up to my father's expectations of me. But, with you by my side, I know I can be better, be the man worthy of becoming Earl and taking over the family fortune and name."

"Please stop, sir," Eliza begged, pulling as hard as she could to get free of Martin's grip. He held her fast, his contrite and apologetic look falling away as his eyes began to widen and his lip curled. He looked like an angered bull in a field being goaded to charge.

"Why, why should you think to reject me? I can offer you everything you could ever want in life. You would be a lady, elevated to the highest pinnacles of society. You would have more than even Edward could ever have hoped to offer you. How... How can you have the gall and nerve to reject me?" Martin rose to his feet, his hand now holding Eliza's wrist in a vice-like grip so she could not escape him.

"You have no real care for me. Whatever you may have told yourself about my fixing you, it is a lie. I do not believe for one moment you want me to improve you and I certainly don't believe that you have any real care for me. If you did care for me or for your brother, you would at least think to show some propriety and give me time to digest the news of Edward's death! Do you really think I could hear such news and then welcome a proposal from you, the man who conspired to send Edward away in the first place? You are insane to believe I might ever have said yes to you."

Martin's grip tightened on Eliza and his free hand moved into the pocket of his coat. Eliza's eyes widened as she saw a flash of silvery metal from within the inner pockets. A pistol. "You had to make this difficult didn't you," Martin cursed as he pulled the gun and pressed it to Eliza's temple. "You're as stubborn a pain in my side as my stupid brother. But I will not let you two beat me, I will not let you both rob me of what is rightfully mine, not without ruining your lives in return." Martin spat the words in Eliza's face.

"What are you talking about?" Eliza cried, struggling even harder to break free of Martin's grip.

"All I have heard this past two years is how much of a disappointment I was, how much my father wished I could be like Edward. Even when I took on the duties of the house, I heard only criticism and scorn. As if Edward could do any better, he was not born to this! He is not the eldest."

Eliza struggled harder now as Martin's voice rose. He was clearly insane, driven mad with jealousy and some desperation. "Please, let go! You are not yourself."

"No, I am exactly who I have always been," Martin returned. "I am Martin Stanford, and apparently that is not enough for the world anymore." His look softened for a moment, regret and pain clearly evident in his face as he drew a deep breath. "Father has made it clear I am not fit to take on his rank and title when the time comes. Breaking with tradition and the divine rights of succession, he has named Edward as the heir! Edward, even after all I did to sour his opinion of my brother."

"He has named Edward? Then... then Edward is not dead?"

Eliza, Despite the fear and danger in which she found herself felt only relief in that instant. Edward was alive and, though her own life was in danger, her spirit lifted to know the man she loved was well and safe.

"Yes, Edward's alive," Martin spat. "I did all I could to make my father denounce him. I had the steward intercept his letters to make it seem as though he had forgotten the family and cared nothing for us."

"You would be so cruel? To your brother? To your mother? Don't you care how greatly we have all feared for him? And..." Eliza paused as a new suspicion entered her mind. "You! You intercepted my letters! Edward never stopped writing to me!"

"Yes, I took them all," Martin returned, his voice laden with bile. "Once I had charge of our family's affairs, I went through all the mail that was sent to us and to the servants. I wanted to keep my brother's letters from reaching my mother and father but I was also keen to make sure my creditors did not try to reach them. When I noticed the letters addressed to you, it did not take much to figure out who "Peter" was. One reading of the notes was enough for me to know that you were in secret correspondence with my brother, and I made sure all letters addressed to you never reached you. I could not have you going to my mother and telling her you had news of Edward... and it was such a thrill to read his letters to you, watching him despair as you failed to answer him over and over and over."

That was enough. Any fear that had kept Eliza frozen in place dissipated at Martin's foul words. The idea that he had robbed her of her letters, that he had made her question Edward's feelings for her, she could not let such a crime go unanswered. Forgetting even the gun pressed to her head, Eliza lashed out, striking Martin in the face with her free hand.

A shot fired, Martin pulling the trigger on reflex as he staggered backwards, clutching his nose. Eliza shrieked, jumping as the glass window behind her shattered. A rush of cold air entered the room, and she looked out into the dark of the night and then to Martin. He staggered about, swearing and cursing as he lifted his pistol. Eliza knew she could not tarry or linger. Picking up her skirts, she ran toward the shattered window, jumping over the broken glass and falling face-first into the snow as the hem of her dress caught on the jagged edges. It was a blessing in disguise. As she fell into the snow another bark of gunfire filled the air, Martin's second shot sailing past her into the night. He was looking to kill her. Eliza was certain of it.

Pushing up onto her feet, heedless of the cold, Eliza pushed forward into the dark. She could hear Martin moving after her, another shot firing into the night as he pursued her into the grounds and toward the fens.

CHAPTER 9

Eliza's breath came in ragged gasps and her pace was failing. Though she knew she needed to keep ahead of her pursuer, though she knew her life depended on it, her body could only be pushed so far.

Martin was relentless in his pursuit. He had followed her out onto the grounds of the estate, goading her with dire threats and jeers as they pushed out onto the frozen fens where Eliza had once worked so many years ago.

"You know you should have just agreed to marry me," Martin shouted into the dark as Eliza rested for a moment behind the cover of a dead and bent willow. "It didn't need to come to this. If you'd just done what any sensible girl would in your shoes, we could have come out of this as husband and wife, and I would have my leverage to get back my title and name when Edward returned home."

Eliza gritted her teeth, at last feeling like she understood the madness that had driven Martin to her. He could not bear the thought of Edward taking his inheritance and future from him, so he looked to repay the indignity by robbing Edward of something, someone precious to him. It made Eliza sick to think of it and she was pleased that she had been able to thwart Martin's plans.

"I suppose, if I can't use you as a bargaining chip to make Edward surrender what is mine back to me, I can at least deprive him of that which he holds dear." Martin's calls were designed to inspire fear in her, to make her reveal herself. In the dark and gloom, Eliza was sure Martin could not see her. He was trying to coax her out of hiding, trying to bait her out.

"You should have seen the things he wrote you in his letter near the end," Martin continued. "I was tempted to show them to mother and father. If it weren't that revealing the letters would have exposed my intercepting the mail to them, I reckon one glance at them would have been enough to horrify them both." Martin's voice changed to a mocking, lilting impersonation of his brother filling the air. "Why won't you write back to me, Eliza. Could it be you have found happiness with some other man? Eliza, I know it is unseemly to express this in a mere letter, but I must confess my true feelings to you now. I hope, revealing the depths of my regard and love for you will spur you to write to me again, to at least explain why it is you now shun me as you do."

Eliza's breathing deepened, her frozen hands balling into fists as she heard the words. It was the strangest sensation in the world. She felt happiness, a delight to hear the feelings that she had so long harboured for Edward were returned, and deep, seething anger at her letters being withheld from her, at having to hear Edward's love for her through Martin's foul teasing. She knew the man was close now, his voice louder and his boots crunching on the frozen mud nearby. She braced herself, knowing she must soon run or fight. She knew the fens well, knew it was dangerous to press too deep into the bog in the dark of night. Even as a child, back when she knew the ways and paths, she would not have dared venture into the fens at night. Already, deep pools of frozen water surrounded her on her left and right. The dry earth about her feet was quickly giving way to mud and she could hear water churning as Martin occasionally missed his footing and his boot struck the water either side of him.

She could not run.

Looking about her, Eliza noticed something on the ground by her foot. A fallen branch from the dead tree. Though scared for her life and knowing she had barely a chance of fighting Martin Stanford, she knelt down, quiet as she could, and picked up the wood.

"Seems fitting, doesn't it, ending our acquaintance out here in the swamp," Martin continued, his voice very close now. "The leech collector returns to where she belongs, soon to be devoured by the bloodsuckers she used to dredge up from the mud. Just think, if you had just kept yourself here where you belonged, we wouldn't be in this situation. It's your own fault you have to die here… it's your fault I'm reduced to this." Martin's anger seeped into his voice again. Eliza gripped the branch she held tighter, breathing a silent prayer that she would not miss her opportunity when Martin rounded the tree and found her.

Her eyes well-adjusted to the gloom, Eliza could see a boot moving out from around the corner. She did not wait for Martin to present himself fully. With a scream, she pushed out from her cover, swinging the broken branch she held with all the might she could muster. It hit Martin square in the chest, and his shadow doubled over as he let out a cry of pain. The wood broke to pieces and Eliza's eyes widened in fear as she realised her only means of defence was lost to her. Pushing out from her cover, she looked to pass Martin while he was bent over, but a hand reached out and grabbed her arm, keeping her pinned to the spot.

"You'll pay for that," Martin growled, his other hand grasping for Eliza and finding her waist. Eliza realised Martin must have dropped the pistol when she struck him, and she writhed and bucked to free herself from his grasp. Without his gun, she could escape him. Without a pistol, she had a chance.

Together, the pair wrestled and lurched over the uneven ground. Martin sought to pull Eliza down onto the dirt below, Eliza thrashed and tossed her weight every which way, not caring if she plunged both of them into the icy waters of the fens.

"I am not letting you walk away. You don't get to walk away from me!" Martin's words were laced with venom, and Eliza could feel his strength overpowering her. No matter how she tried, she could not shrug the man from her, nor could she throw him into the mire. Her eyes looked out in the dark, the faint glow of light from Stanford Manor the only comfort, a last comfort before Martin inevitably overpowered her. Though she would fight to her last breath, some part of Eliza accepted that she would not survive this encounter.

"Martin! Martin, stop!" A voice in the dark caught Eliza's ear and she peered out into the gloom, swearing she recognised it. Another sound rang out in the night, a gunshot that barked out across the fens and succeeded in bringing Martin Stanford to heel.

"Let go of her, Martin. If you put even one scratch on Eliza, I will end you, and I assure you, those years I spent languishing in the regiments have made me quite the capable shot, even in the dark."

Eliza's mouth fell open, and she felt her heart lift as she recognised the voice, realised who her saviour was striding through the gloom.

"Edward!" Eliza called his name, trying to break free and rush toward him. Martin still held her by the wrist though, unwilling to let her go even if he had ceased his attempt to throw her into the bogs.

"So, you came straight here from the boat? I should have figured you'd come running straight to the leech girl and not to our parents. I wonder how Father will take the news."

"Still hoping he might reinstate you as heir?" Edward asked, stepping closer through the gloom. He held a lantern in one hand, Eliza able to make out his proud, handsome face as he looked to his brother. Dressed in the bold red of Her Majesty's army, he looked every bit the hero and Eliza doubted Martin would dare oppose his younger brother now.

"We can let our parents decide our fates when we return to London," Edward said, his voice calm but authoritative. "I promise you this though, if you lay even a finger on Eliza, if you do not let her go right now, I will not hesitate to shoot you down."

"You don't have the nerve," Martin spat. Eliza turned, looking to Martin in fear. She had been certain the man would see reason when looking down the barrel of a gun, but even now his hatred toward Edward, his bilious indignation at the way his life had turned, held sway over him. She saw Martin looking down at his feet, noticing the pistol that he had dropped when she had struck him.

"I'll let her go," Martin said, at last, his voice poisonous like a viper. "I'll let her go to you and then I want you both to lower your weapon. I don't want to risk you trying to off me once I lose my leverage."

"Whatever happened to my not having the nerve?" Edward returned.

"Don't play games with me, Edward, I have had a bad year, and I need only one more excuse to take out my anger on dear Eliza here."

Edward put up his hands, immediately raising his pistol. "You've made your point, Martin. Let her go and I will drop it."

Martin smirked, releasing Eliza and shoving her roughly forward. As good as his word, Edward immediately dropped his weapon.

"Edward, he has a gun!" Eliza screamed as she was thrown forward. She hit the frozen earth hard, looking back in terror as Martin dove to the floor and grabbed his pistol. She tried to push up onto her feet, to throw herself in Martin's way, but a shadow rushed past her. Eliza's eyes widened as the shadow of Edward flew past her, barrelling into Martin before he could aim his pistol. Both brothers rolled over in the muck and Eliza froze as she heard an almighty splash.

"Edward! Edward!" Eliza screamed his name, rushing forward on her hands and knees in the dark to the stretch of water where the two brothers had fallen in. She could not see either man, but she could hear their thrashing about below the waterline. Still on her knees, she plunged her hands into the water, feeling through the gloom for a hand, a lapel, anything she could latch onto. Something passed between her fingers, and she latched onto it, throwing her weight backward for all she was worth.

"Come on Edward, please be you," she breathed as she yanked the man free from the waters. If she had found Martin, if Edward was still below the waterline, then all hopes of rescuing him might be gone. Martin would leave him for dead, throwing her into the mire too just to satisfy his insane jealousy and rage.

In the darkness, it was impossible to make out the features of the man who lay coughing and spluttering on the banks. Eliza gritted her teeth, hands wiping his face and peering through the dark for a sign.

"Edward! Edward, is it you?"

"It's... It's me!" Edward managed to reply between gasps.

Eliza let out a grateful sob, throwing her arms about him and hugging him tightly. Edward did not reciprocate though. As soon as he had recovered his breath, he moved to the edge of the bank, worry and fear gripping him. "Martin! Martin."

Eliza moved out of the way, watching as Edward plunged his hands into the water as she had done. She did not stop him. Martin, for all his faults, was family to Edward.

"Come on Martin, you're not getting out of this so easy," Edward growled. He began to push back, and Eliza could make out in the dark that he had something. Rallying her courage and wanting to do what was best for the man she loved, she moved to his side and helped pull Martin to the shore.

"Is... Is he alive?" Eliza asked, her voice frightened lest the still body jump suddenly to life and attack them again.

Edward leaned over the body, pressing his hand to Martin's chest and another to his neck.

"He's still breathing, just unconscious." Edward looked up toward Eliza. "Are you hurt? Did Martin injure you?"

"I'm fine," Eliza assured him, and she truly meant it. In his presence at that moment, all the pain and fear she had endured dissipated, the relief and joy at having her friend returned to her dispelling all else. "I am so glad you're alive, Edward. Martin... he told me so many things, made me think you had died."

She could hear Edward's breath hitch in the dark. "My brother has a lot to answer for, and it seems we both have much to catch up on, but we can't linger out here in the cold."

Eliza nodded. Stepping awkwardly on her feet, she helped steady Edward as he lifted his unconscious brother onto his shoulders.

"I didn't think you'd be saving me from the swamp again in this lifetime," Edward mused jokingly as they limped quietly through the dark. Eliza smiled and shook her head.

"I guess this means you owe me another necklace."

CHAPTER 10

"I still can't believe it," Edward said, shaking his head as he stared into the fire. "I mean, I can see it. I know my brother and I know he is capable of everything you said, but still... to ride here begging for you to marry him just to score a measure of revenge on me."

"I am more astounded that he ever thought such a thing could work," Eliza said, offering a wan smile and reaching over to take Edward's hand. "You should have seen his expression when I rejected him. I have never seen such anger. The look in his eyes, it'll haunt me for the rest of my days, I swear."

"I am sorry you faced so harrowing an ordeal," Edward said, his thumb tracing a line over the back of Eliza's hand as they sat under a shared blanket by the fire. "Martin has had his way all his life, always given whatever he wanted and been indulged when he should have been disciplined.

It should come as no great shock that he could not handle his emotions when at last my mother and father looked to correct him or threaten to take that which he thought should rightly be his."

On return to Stanford Manor, Edward and Eliza were met by the servants who had remained on the grounds. They were brought to the house and installed in the library, a roaring fire made up and blankets and fresh clothes brought to them. Both were covered in mud, Edward's skin mottled with crusted muck all over. Hot baths were already being drawn for them both and Isabelle was looking to make some kind of meal from the provisions left in the kitchens. As for Martin, he was taken to his room and locked inside. On Edward's orders, he was stripped of his wet things and attended to, so he did not succumb to hypothermia. Beyond this though, Martin was afforded no favours, and two servants were placed outside his door as guards as they waited for the doctor and the local officers of the law in Denton to come up to the manor and take care of him.

"What will your parents make of all this?" Eliza asked. "I mean, you almost killed your brother, over me."

"I saved him too," Edward replied with a shrug. He looked to Eliza, resolve in his face as he looked into her eyes. "In truth, I do not much care what mother and father do after this. When a letter reached me from my mother, explaining that my father wished me to inherit the estate and she feared their letters to us weren't reaching me, I knew I had to come home at once. After a year of silence, it seemed mother realised Martin must have been keeping my letters from her and ensuring her letters to me did not reach me either. I had thought it strange, especially to receive nothing from you, but it was only when my mother's own had reached me that I realised the games my brother had been playing and the need to come home."

"But you came here to me... before seeing your own parents?" Eliza spoke, the words whispered in wonder.

"Of course, I came to you first," Edward said, his smile growing deeper as he let go of Eliza's hand and instead brushed her cheek. "When I stopped receiving your letters, I fell into something of a panic. I began to suspect all sorts of things, feared that you had fallen in love with one of the other servants or perhaps some man from the village. I convinced myself that you had become caught up in some new happiness and had forgotten me."

"That is absurd. You know I couldn't do that," Eliza assured him. Even as she spoke, she reflected on the many fears and imaginings she had endured over the last year and chuckled. "... I suppose I can't censure you though. When Martin started intercepting your letters to me, my first jealous thought was that you had fallen in love with an exotic girl from overseas."

"You were jealous?" Edward asked, his smile turning into a grin. Eliza smirked back, nudging his shoulder playfully.

"Don't go stoking that ego of yours too much," she teased.

Edward nodded, looking back to the fire and taking a deep breath. "Joking aside, the absence of letters from you, my fears that you had fallen in love with some other man, forced me to confront feelings I had long harboured and, to my shame, resisted for too long."

"Martin may have mentioned something of them, but I would like to hear them from your own lips," Eliza said with a soft smile, her arm moving about Edward as they huddled together side by side.

"It was just as I thought I was set to lose you that I realised that I loved you. I knew then with absolute certainty that the difference in our circumstances, the disapproval of my parents, all of it meant nothing to me. I began to write to you almost daily, begging you to hear me out. I began to make a nuisance of myself to the high command, demanding I return to England on an urgent matter. My request was always denied, and I only received the proper dispensation when my mother's letter reached me. With my father looking to change his will, my brother leaving our house and name in disgrace, and my father's health failing, I was at last given leave to return to England. I looked to keep my return a secret, but somehow Martin must have learned of the letter mother sent to me. It was surely that which convinced him to come here tonight to make his desperate attempt at marrying you. If he saw the letters that I wrote to you, he would have known my only true goal in returning home was to find you and tell you how I truly feel... that I love you."

Words failed Eliza at that moment. Hearing the sentiment she had so long wanted to hear and never believed would be uttered to her, she could not help drawing close to Edward, her eyes locked on his as their lips closed inch by inch, both trembling.

"You... You do not know how many times I have replayed that kiss we shared all those years ago. I rushed away in such a fluster, but I always wished... I always wanted to one day return to you and kiss you as I did that night."

"I want that too. It is what I have wanted more than anything," Eliza whispered back, their faces so close now she could feel Edward's warm breath on her skin.

Fingers moved through her hair, Edward's rough, strong hands drawing her in, as if she needed any coaxing or guidance. Eliza's eyes closed, and her heart swelled with joy as their lips connected as she became lost in the sensation of Edward. Her own hands moved about him, holding him so tight lest he should disappear into thin air and this moment of joy cruelly reveal itself to be nought but a dream. But Edward remained. They continued to kiss and hold one another, years of mutual longing and repressed desire making itself known as they found themselves at last reunited. Any pain or suffering caused them by Martin was forgotten in that instant, his dark shadow that had loomed over both their lives dispelled as they found one another. God's light had broken through with a pure love, tested and tried in the furnace.

Time passed in a haze and Eliza only became aware of the outside world again when a creaking was heard behind them, and she noticed a shadow at the door. She drew back from Edward then, blushing profusely as Isabelle watched them both with a poorly concealed smile on her lips. "Sorry to interrupt, My Lord, but I thought you should know that both your baths have been drawn. It is probably best you take them to ensure you do not catch a chill."

Colour rose to Edward's cheek, and he sighed as he looked at Eliza. "I believe we have time to continue this conversation later. I will not be disappearing or leaving your side again, ever."

Eliza nodded, reluctantly letting the man help her to her feet. She watched as Edward walked away into the hall, attended to by one of the male servants. Eliza was left alone with Isabelle whose grin was now so wide it seemed to stretch full about her face.

"You must tell me everything!" Isabelle squealed, Eliza letting out a sigh as she followed her friend toward the bath. Though trying to pretend to be irked by the interruption, she could not disguise her joy at having, at last, had her feelings answered. She truly longed to tell Isabelle everything, to have the whole world know. There would be those who would criticise and raise their eyebrows, but she cared not. She had Edward back, and he was not going to leave her again. As long as she had that, nothing else in the world mattered.

EPILOGUE

Christmas 1855

Eliza could never have hoped to be recognized by Lord and Lady Stanford. She knew from the moment she had accepted Edward's proposal that she could not reasonably expect his parents to be pleased with the match. At the same time, she knew she did not need their blessing. So long as she had Edward's, she was content.

Lord Stanford was not pleased to see his youngest son return to him, engaged to a servant of the manor, but his qualms at Edward's choice in wife paled in comparison to Martin's crimes. When Edward explained all that had happened at the manor, Martin's attempt at marrying Eliza, then attempting to kill her, it left his father with no choice but to disinherit and disown his wayward son.

Martin himself was tried in the courts for the attempted murder and forced to account for a great deal of debt he had accumulated over the last year. His sentence was severe, Lord Stanford refusing to mitigate any prison time his son had earned by paying fines for him.

With Martin jailed and disgraced and Edward determined to marry the servant who had rescued him from the fens so many years ago, the old and tired Earl had only two choices before him—to accept Edward's marriage and grant him the land and titles that would have gone to Martin, or else let the name of Stanford fall into obscurity with his death. Unsurprisingly, the Earl chose the lesser of the two evils and gave his begrudging consent for Edward to marry in the March following his return to England.

Sadly, the Earl did not survive long enough to see Edward married, though Eliza felt this might have been a blessing to the old man who so detested the idea of his son marrying beneath his station. With Edward named Earl, Eliza found herself made his Countess. In the months following their marriage, Edward's mother warmed to the union. When it became quite clear that their friends and neighbours weren't gossiping about Eliza, when she knew her invitations to certain parties hadn't been affected by the union, she became quite civil about the whole matter, even declaring herself rather fond of Eliza.

With his new duties as Earl to consider, Edward bought out his commission from the army, receiving an honourable discharge that freed him from the career he had never wanted for himself. In the months following his marriage, he dedicated himself to fulfilling those dreams and ambitions Eliza had helped foster in him during his youth. He looked to create his own business, clawing back the family fortunes through wise investments in the steel and the growing rail industry. It would take years for all the harm Martin had done to the family finances to be wiped clean, but Edward proved himself more than capable of the task and earned praise in all quarters of London as his name became synonymous with good sense and prudent investment.

～

As Christmas morning rose over the world, Eliza sat up in bed. It was still very dark outside, the hour not yet four. She lit a candle, the action causing her husband to stir in his bed. He opened an eye, smiling a little as he looked at his wife. "You know, there is no need for you to be awake. How long will it take for you to realise you can linger in bed with me?"

"I have spent my entire life rising before the sun," Eliza said. "It's you who are the lazy one. You should try getting up with me rather than lounging in bed till eight. So much of the day is lost by then."

Edward sat up a little, an amused smirk on his lips. "Who are you calling lazy? You should see the times I had to wake up while I was serving oversees. I am more than capable of getting up at this hour with you… I just wish we could stay in bed a little longer."

Eliza smiled, leaning in to kiss Edward. "Well, I was going to go down to the servants' kitchens and join them for breakfast. I made sure they all had an extra special treat this year to make up for everything we've endured in the last years. I would like to remind them that I do not consider myself so far removed from them just because I am the Lady of the house."

Edward nodded. "A fine idea. Do you think they would find it strange if I joined you?"

"I am sure it would ruffle a few feathers, but our marriage has already done that. At least dining with your staff will be seen by them as a mark in your favour. Not that they needed any more reason to approve of you. You are already a more generous master than your father or Martin ever were."

"I fear that is not a high bar to surpass," Edward joked as he rolled out of bed and began to dress. Eliza was a little slower, holding her slightly swollen belly as she moved over to the dresser.

"Are you all right?" Edward asked, noticing as his wife's breathing became a little laboured.

"Our child is just excited, they must know it is Christmas," Eliza said with a smile.

"They take after their mother," Edward said approvingly, "Always eager to greet the day early."

Husband and wife smiled at once another, then returned to dressing to greet the Christmas day.

The high praise lifted in church later that morning, as believers gathered to welcome and worship their Saviour, sounded like choirs of angels to Eliza's ears. How far she had come. As she sang the wonderful truths of redemption rang through her being.

"He brought me up also out of an horrible pit, out of the miry clay, and set my feet upon a rock..." (Psalm 40:2)

∽

THANK YOU FOR CHOOSING A PUREREAD BOOK!

We hope you enjoyed the story, and as a way to thank you for choosing PureRead we'd like to send you this free book, and other fun reader rewards…

Click here for your free copy of Whitechapel Waif
PureRead.com/victorian

Thanks again for reading.
See you soon!

HAVE YOU READ?

THE ORPHAN PICKPOCKET'S CHRISTMAS

I'm certain that Eliza's story has blessed your socks off!

What an unforgettable journey from the cold swampy marshes to the warm embrace of true love.

If you love stories that lift troubled souls from despair to joy, you'll definitely want to dive into Jess Weir's new Christmas Victorian family saga, *The Orphan Pickpocket's Christmas*.

In the heart of 1875 Victorian London, where the city's ruthless streets guard the darkest of secrets, two orphaned souls stand defiant in the face of adversity...

For your enjoyment here are the first chapters of Emma's heartrending tale...

VICTORIAN ROMANCE

THE ORPHAN PICKPOCKET'S CHRISTMAS

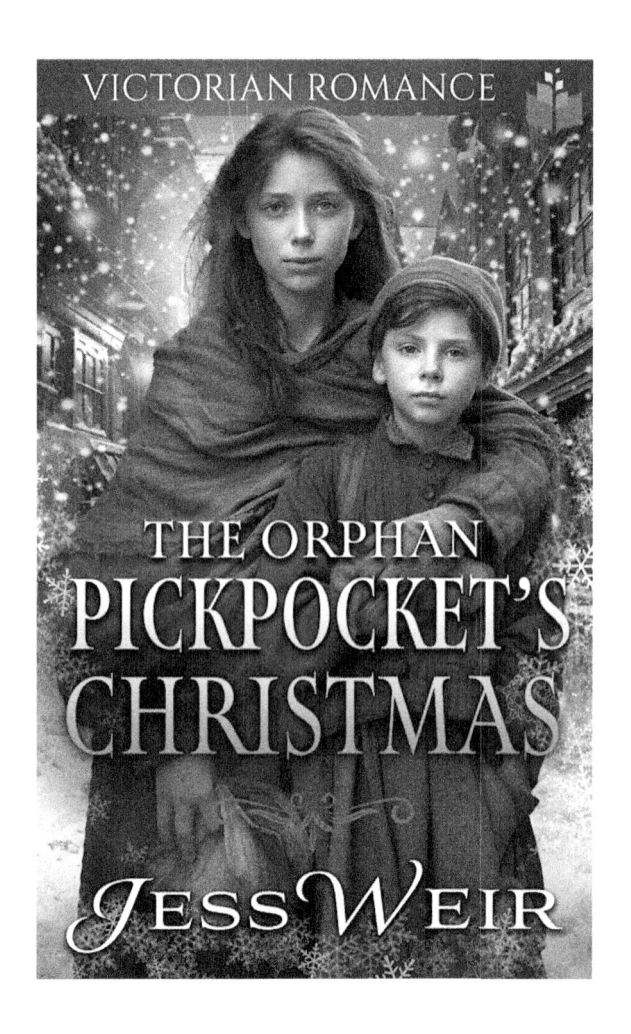

Jess Weir

Emma Mason walked along the street and stared at the beautiful dresses of the women who bustled around the market. They were like proud peacocks, displaying their feathers for all the world to see. It made Emma sad. Once she had worn beautiful dresses, or at least nice dresses, but that was before Papa left. He had been gone for over six years now and things were getting slowly worse. The dress she wore was worn in places and had been extended with a hem of contrasting material to keep up with her growth. She would soon be sixteen and hoped that her mama would allow her to get a new gown.

As she had the thought, they passed a milliner's shop. In the window was the most delightful bonnet. It was light blue with pink edging. The blue lace was weaved through with pink ribbon. For a moment Emma imagined what it would feel like to wear it. Of course, with a matching dress. She would hold her head high and walk down the street smiling at every handsome boy who gave her a wink.

Of course, Mama would never let her have such a beautiful hat, never mind a dress that would go with it, but she could dream. As always, when she dreamed of something better, she thought of their papa.

"When is Papa coming home?" she asked her mother who walked along at her side hauling the basket with the goods from the market.

Pamela Mason sighed. "How many times have I told you child, that I don't want to talk about it?"

"But, Mama, I only have my memories and they are fading. Will you tell me a little about him?" Emma had hoped that her mother would soften one day. She had asked this same question, or others like it a thousand times and it either made her mother angry or withdrawn.

Emma thought that she was probably sad but that she didn't want to admit it. That was why she snapped and changed the subject.

"Watch where you're walking," Pamela said.

Emma held her foot in mid-air, just in time to avoid a rather nasty looking puddle. Runoff from the butchers had congealed into a horrid mess that was buzzing with flies and would have stained the hem of her dress. Stepping over, Emma wondered if she should try again. She was feeling bold as she had seen the small rabbit that her mama had haggled for in the market. They would have meat in their stew tonight.

"When will he be back?" Emma asked.

Another sigh. "Benedict is gone, let's just leave it that way."

"Did he abandon us, Mama?" Emma always felt hurt. It was as if her mother was trying to protect her and her memories of her papa. It always made her wonder if he had run off with someone else. Had he found someone prettier than her mama and her? Did he get tired of her brother David's crying? The boy was nine now but he was still young when Papa left. Why would he abandon them? They used to have a nice house. Now they lived in two rooms of a tenement, in a slum close to the Old Nicol. Surely, he loved them too much to leave them to this?

"Stop asking questions. Your papa loved you and he had to go away. You know that is all I will say on this."

"But, Mama, if he loved us…"

The sound of a scuffle broke out followed by shouting.

"Thief, thief, stop that boy."

The sound of the Peelers' whistles echoed around the market place followed by running footsteps that rumbled across the cobblestones.

Emma peered through the crowds trying to get a better look. A young boy, he looked about Emma's age perhaps a little older, had tried to take a gold pocket watch. The fine gentleman had pushed him over and shouted *thief*. Only, the boy was quick and got to his feet weaving in and out of the crowds as the larger but more ungainly police tried to catch him. He passed by Emma and her mother, and Emma and he locked eyes. It only lasted for a split second, but it felt a lot longer. He had such a look of shame on his face, and his eyes seemed to beg forgiveness from her. As soon as he had come, he was gone, scampering off into the crowd and to freedom.

"You must never steal," Pamela said in her most stern voice. It was her second rule, the first being that no one should ask about their father. "Bad things happen to thieves. They go to the gallows or are taken away. Never steal, no matter how bad it gets. Do you hear me, girl?"

Emma pulled her eyes away from the crowd. This time the boy had escaped. A vision of his dirty cheeks and the mud caked knees that showed below his trousers came to her mind. Why would he do such a thing?

"Come now, girl, let's get home and prepare this lovely rabbit," Pamela said.

Emma smiled and wondered how long it would last them. Her stomach rumbled as she realized it had been over a week since they had eaten any meat. For now, she put the thoughts of her father behind her and wondered how she could help them now. Maybe she could get a job. Mama worked in service at a big house just an hour's walk away from their home. Perhaps they would take her on. Across the market she saw a handsome man selling veg. Then there was her favourite dream. Perhaps she would find a rich and handsome man to marry her and all their problems would be over.

"Stop dawdling, girl," Pamela said. "I want to get home to remind your brother what happens to thieves."

∽

Soon, they were walking down dirtier, and smellier streets. Emma only noticed the smell when she came back into the slum that was now her home. It was the smell of outhouses and dead cats. Of discarded rubbish and decay, but you soon got used to it. A rat ran along the building before them. For a moment, it stopped and turned to look back. Its beady black eyes stared like death and Emma shuddered. She had once heard a story that rats would come for you at night and nibble out your eyes. With a flick of its tail it was gone, disappearing into a shrub that grew out of the corner of a house.

"Stop dawdling, girl, I have to pay the rent today."

Emma realized that her mama was still walking and now that the rat had gone, she ran to catch up. Only, another shudder went down her spine. Paying the rent always made Mama anxious. It was rare that they would have meat on rent day… still, the rabbit had been pretty mangled and not too fresh. But it wasn't her mama's anxiety that made her uneasy. What caused this feeling was Jairus Cuthbert. Emma wasn't sure if he owned the building that they and four other families lived in, or if he merely collected the rent. Either way she dreaded seeing him.

As they arrived back at the house, she was hoping to avoid Jairus but that wouldn't happen. The man was leaning against the wall of their building. A pipe in his mouth, one hand on his prominent gut. As they drew nearer, he reached for his pocket watch and shook his head. Mama increased the speed of her walking whilst Emma hung back, hoping to remain unnoticed in her mother's shadow.

It wasn't to be. The landlord licked his slug like lips and his dark beady eyes reminded her of the rat. Running a hand through his slicked-back black hair, a smile came to those abhorrent lips.

"Mrs Mason, I was beginning to think you were not going to pay today," he said, keeping his eyes on Emma.

"I'm sorry, Mr Cuthbert, Emma here has been dawdling today. You know how children have their head in the clouds sometimes," Pamela passed Emma the basket whilst she rummaged in her coin purse.

"That one's no longer a child," Jairus said. "If you struggle with the rent, well, I'm sure we can come to some arrangement. I'm looking for a new wife, since the last one passed on."

"Mr. Cuthbert!"

"Here," Pamela said as she handed over the coins. "That will happen over my dead body."

"Be careful what you wish for." Cuthbert grinned and then stepped aside to let them pass.

∾

Back in their two rooms they found David playing with his wooden train. It was worn now, the paint all rubbed away. It was the last present their father had carved for him before he disappeared and David treasured it like nothing else.

Emma went to sit with her brother for a few minutes. This morning she had scoured the neighbourhood with him for wood. They had found enough scraps to light a small fire. Hopefully, it would be enough to cook the rabbit. Only, Mama was not preparing the meal. Instead, she had removed the loose floorboard in the corner of the room and was counting their coins. There was something about her face that worried Emma.

"What is it, Mama?"

Pamela looked up and shook her head. "It's nothing, child. Help me prepare this rabbit. I have a few carrots and a turnip; we will have us a hearty stew for a few nights. Along with the bread, we will feast like the queen."

Emma felt a flush of joy go through her. What would it be like to feast like the queen? She ruffled David's mop of curly blond hair and left the boy to play while she prepared the vegetables. All the time she dreamed of the handsome man she would marry. How he would buy her fine dresses. They would live in a house with a bath and would eat meat every day. There would be coal to put on the fire and a clean blanket. It put a smile on her face and drove out the chill left by Jairus from earlier.

With the fire lit, and the stew pot hung over it, the rooms were soon filled with a delicious smell. Emma sat on the pallet she shared at night with her mama while David played with his train. Emma wanted to keep dreaming but she knew something was wrong.

"Mama, I was wondering…"

"Yes, child?"

"Maybe I could work with you at the big house… maybe that would make you happier?"

Pamela left the stew and came over to sit down next to her. "I'm not unhappy, child."

"Something is wrong," Emma said, feeling more and more certain that she was right.

"We are just a little short of coin. It is nothing to worry about and you need to look after your brother most days."

"I can manage on my own," David said looking up with the face of an angel and big blue eyes that convinced you he was one.

"I know you can," Pamela said. For a few moments she was quiet and she seemed to be staring at nothing. Her fingers twiddled the wedding band that she still wore. It was a habit she had and Emma doubted she even knew she was doing it.

"I will talk to the housekeeper," Pamela said at last. "If they agree, we will start you on two days a week first and build you up, how does that sound?"

"It sounds great," Emma said. Part of her really wanted to do this. Knew that she was old enough to take some of the burden off her sweet mama, and yet she felt worried that her world was about to change. In her experience, change was never good.

～

It had been two weeks since Emma started working at the big house. The walk there and back took an hour each way and the first time she had loved it. As they gradually came out of the slums the sights, sounds, and smells were even better than the markets. The ladies wore such colourful dresses, the men in their jackets, breeches and top hats were a sight to be seen. So handsome that she wanted to swoon. The girlish part of her wanted one of these men to notice her. To see through her patched dress, and just a few weeks ago, that would be all that was on her mind. Only, she reckoned that she was growing up for a part of her knew that was just childish. Men didn't rescue pretty maidens, not even their fathers.

Then there was the smell, perfume drifted on the air, from the ladies and from flowers that grew in the gardens of the houses. The air was breathable and clean, fresh almost.

The smell of newly cooked bread seemed to fill the air and make her stomach rumble and her mouth salivate.

Horses and carriages of all shapes and sizes were everywhere. The sound of their hooves clip-clopping down the street as the carriage wheels rumbled along behind.

It was like going into a different world, only at night, when she was exhausted, she had to make the long walk home. This time the world gradually got dimmer. The light and bright streets with their now sweet smells of cooking meat and roasting vegetables were replaced with the smell of sewer and things long rotten. On that first walk home she had come to understand her position in life and to realise that it was not good. Once more she had wanted to ask about her papa but it seemed childish and she could see a fatigue in her mother that worried her. As they walked home in silence, she understood that one day her mother would be gone and she wanted to drop down in the dirty street and cry.

That had been two weeks ago and in this short time she had become accustomed to the long hours and hard work. Already she understood the burden her mother had carried and yet Pamela never moaned or mentioned it. In her mind, it just was.

They were halfway through the walk back and Emma could still feel her hands stinging. Monday was wash day. As the new girl she had been given this task. It meant hours of dunking her hands into scalding water and scrubbing until her fingers were raw.

Several times during the day she had seen her mother hovering nearby. It was obvious that she wanted to take over, but that she was resisting. Each time, Emma had thrown her one of her most dazzling smiles. Though she wanted the help, she was determined to do her bit.

The housekeeper's name was Martha Jones, she was a big woman with rosy red cheeks and a face that you expected to smile. It didn't, or at least, not that Emma had seen. Somehow, she didn't think that the woman would like it if her mother helped her. In fact, she wondered if she might even get her mother in trouble. The woman had a temper and didn't mind raising her voice to issue an order. Whenever she did maids, cooks, sculleries, and footmen all ducked their heads and buckled down to work.

All afternoon, the woman had been watching as Emma folded the washed item and brought it all back to the kitchen. It was someone else's job to iron it, which was a big relief. The ever-watching housekeeper made her nervous. So much so, that she was afraid that she might burn something if she was left to use the flat iron. It was a tool she had hardly ever used but she had watched her mother. First, you had to heat it on the stove and then with a cloth, you carefully ironed the clothes. Only, it was a job that required a lot of skill and caution. Otherwise, the beautiful linens and clothing would be ruined.

Emma pushed the thought of the work behind her. It was harder than she expected. In her mind she had imagined making lots of new friends. As it was, she had hardly had time to mutter more than a *hello* to the equally busy maids and scullions. The handsome footmen in their uniforms of black jackets with the shiny buttons had hardly cast her a glance. At first, she thought that they thought her beneath them, but she now realized that they were too busy doing their own jobs to notice one more maid. At least, she too had a uniform just like her mama's. The black dress with the heavily starched white apron was the nicest thing she had worn in many years. Even the bonnet made her feel good as she walked down the street.

Tomorrow she was to work in the kitchen. Preparing the potatoes and washing pots as well as scrubbing the floor and general cleaning. Maybe then she would have more time to get to know her new workmates.

"You're very quiet," her mother said as they walked past the now closed market.

"Sorry, I was thinking."

"If it's too much for you, we can try to find you something easier," Pamela added.

"No, Mama, it's not that." Emma wanted to stop the work, but she was beginning to understand that they needed the money. She was also beginning to understand the looks that Jairus gave her and what they meant. She was even beginning to understand that they could end up worse than they were. Going to the big house with all its luxuries had not made her feel worse about her current situation. It had, in fact, made her realise just how lucky she was. For each morning and night as they walked the long road to and from work, she saw the poor. People sleeping in corners and begging for bread. How could she not have seen it before? "I like the job… I'm just a little tired is all." Emma had found the lie came easily to her lips but she could see that her mother believed none of it.

"I think I will talk to Mrs Jones, see if I can get you an easier position," Pamela said.

Emma nearly shouted *no*; she remembered Mrs Jones telling her that this was not a free ride. Before she got the easy jobs, she had to pay her dues. Somehow, she didn't think the steely old woman would take kindly to her mother asking for favours. So how could she distract her? It came to her right away. What always stopped her mother talking?

"When will you tell me more about Papa?" Emma said in a slightly more childish voice. One that was bound to annoy her mother.

"There is nothing to tell. He isn't here and you must remember that he's not coming back."

"Why?" Emma was angry now, maybe because she was tired.

"Because I said so. Now hurry along, David has been alone too long."

With that her mother put her head down, pulled her shawl tighter around her shoulders and increased her stride. She was almost running down the cobblestone street, but what was she running from?

. . .

Continue reading this emotional Christmas saga...

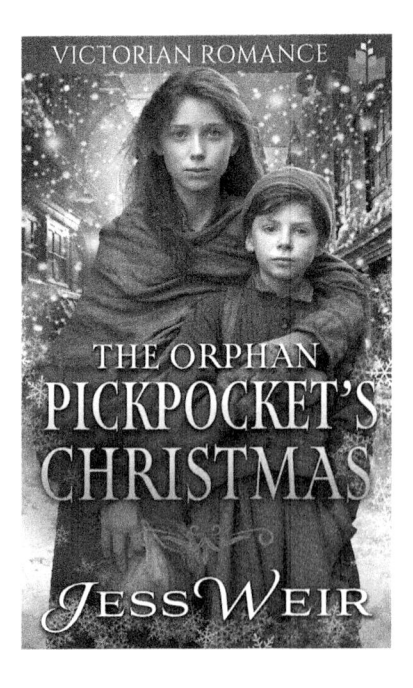

Read The Orphan Pickpocket's Christmas on Amazon

LOVE VICTORIAN CHRISTMAS SAGA ROMANCE?

If you enjoyed this story why not continue straight away with other books in our PureRead Victorian Christmas Romance library?

Read them all...

Churchyard Orphan

Orphan Christmas Miracle

Workhouse Girl's Christmas Dream

The Winter Widow's Daughter

The Match Girl & The Lost Boy's Christmas Hope

The Christmas Convent Child

The Orphan Girl's Winter Secret

Rag And Bone Winter Hope

Isadora's Christmas Plight

PLUS THESE BRAND NEW CHRISTMAS TALES
FROM OUR BESTSELLING VICTORIAN
ROMANCE AUTHORS

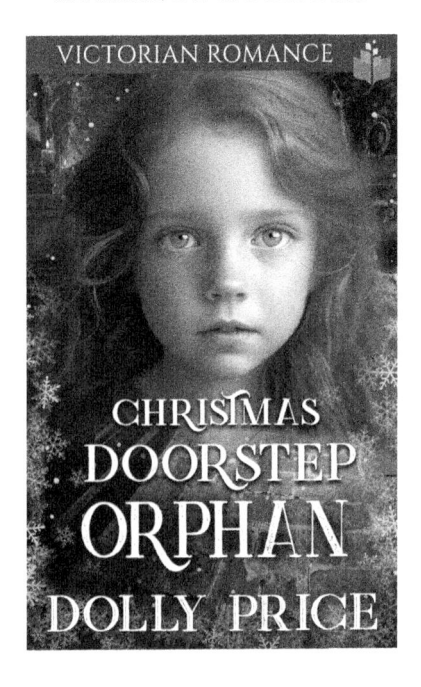

Read Christmas Doorstep Orphan on Amazon

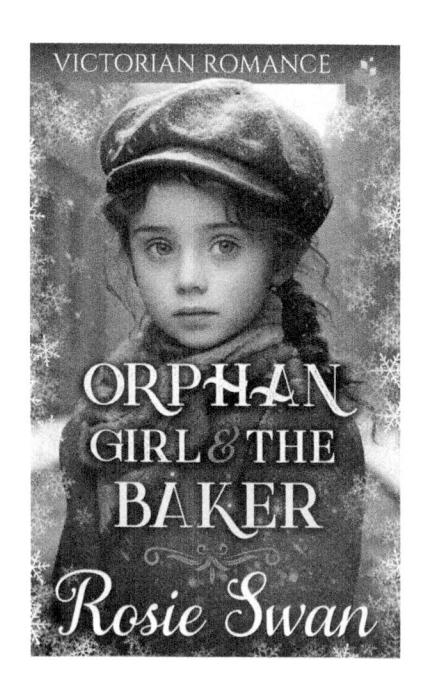

Read Orphan Girl & The Baker on Amazon

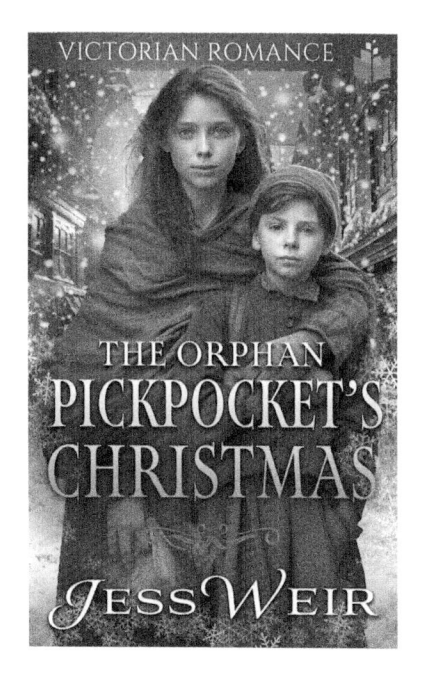

Read The Orphan Pickpocket's Christmas

A Christmas Song For The Prestwich Orphan

OUR GIFT TO YOU

AS A WAY TO SAY THANK YOU WE WOULD LOVE TO SEND YOU THIS BEAUTIFUL STORY FREE OF CHARGE.

Click here for your free copy of Whitechapel Waif

PureRead.com/victorian

At PureRead we publish books you can trust. Great tales without smut or swearing, but with all of the mystery and romance you expect from a great story.

Be the first to know when we release new books, take part in our fun competitions, and get surprise free books in your inbox by signing up to our free VIP Reader list.

As a welcome gift you'll receive the story of the Whitechapel Waif straight to your inbox...

Click here for your free copy of Whitechapel Waif

PureRead.com/victorian

Printed in Great Britain
by Amazon